PERILOUS PIED PIPER

BIG BAD DEEDS SERIES
ROSE SINCLAIR

This is a work of fiction. Names, characters, places, and incidents either are the product of the author's imagination or are used fictitiously. Any resemblance to actual persons, living or dead, events, or locales is entirely coincidental.

Art Over Chaos Publishing
artoverchaos.com

CHAPTER ONE
- PIPER -

I feared the deck of a ship was where I'd end up lost to history. The *Jolly Roger* was full of pirates and an unkillable Captain, which made this the best place for me to keep my share of the bounty. Even better than outright gold, I had earned a favor from the Captain. I had reunited him with the love of his life. It was the easiest job ever since they had been fated for each other all along. But that didn't mean I wanted to spend forever in a dead-end job playing music to calm the seas.

As I sat on a stair between decks, the ship's first mate, Smee, glared daggers at me. She must have seen that my role of matchmaker was a ruse to get a free ride. Since we'd reach the port of Hamelin by evening, that hardly mattered. The ship pitched, and I grabbed the railing to hold on. No one else even wavered in their steps.

"You alright there?" a voice called.

I looked up to see Warren poised a step above me. His shape was merely a silhouette from the sunlight, but I recognized the strum of magic within him as much as the sound of his voice. Before I could even answer, someone else yelled, "Land, ho!"

Warren stepped off the stairs and turned to reach a hand out to me. He was my friend, and I knew I shouldn't push the gesture off, but the newest pirate adapted so fast to a life at sea that I was frankly vexed over it.

"Here is where you wanted to go?" Warren asked as he turned to the smudge of land on the horizon.

I nodded, opening my mouth to answer before another shout cut me off again.

"Captain! You need to see this," yelled a pirate as he leaned over the side of the ship. For a moment, I thought he was going to be sick. But, as more people rushed over, I knew it must have been something else.

Only Warren didn't move, and we both silently tried to figure things out from where we stood. The Captain stepped onto the deck, gesturing with a metal hook for people to clear a path. His mismatched eyes followed the sign sticking up past the waterline as the ship sailed past. Then, he turned to me with a dark gaze. It was a dangerous enough glare that I was tempted to hide behind his lover next to me.

"What is it, Cap'n?" Warren asked.

"It's a plague warning." The focused gaze briefly calmed as he answered Warren. When it settled back on me, it held an accusation. "Did you know this?"

"No!" I liked to goof around, but I'd never risk another's life for profit. I pulled out a rolled piece of parchment from my bag that showed a rat-catcher was wanted. With a shake, I held it out to the Captain to take. "Just says the city is offering 1,000 fucking guilders."

Impressed whistles from scattered crew stole my attention as I looked over pirates who already seemed to count the payday. It was a job worth three years' pay if one were to live large—nearly six if one preferred a more average life.

I knew paying 1,000 guilders to remove some rats had to mean there was some catch, but as a summoner, I hadn't considered it much of a worry. Magic was on my side. I just had to play my pipe, and they'd leave town pestering no one.

The Captain inhaled, chest puffing out as he rolled the flier up and handed it back out. Warren took it first. I silently watched to see whose side he'd be on. The fellow mage wasn't a summoner but a healer. That serendipitous fact could either benefit me or make everything look even more orchestrated.

"The ink on this looks old," Warren said as he pulled it closer to study the lines of a repeated early fold in the paper. "Maybe even issued before there was an outbreak. Or between? If there is still disease in town, I could heal them."

"The rats?" Smee added with a grunt. "Or the people?"

Warren smiled. "Both."

"Ten percent," the Captain said to me, holding his left hand out to shake.

My only thought was to make sure I offered the correct hand in return. As my boss, he had never been a staunch friend, but we worked well together. And the trust he had in Warren went beyond magic and reason. It was love.

Strangers walking into the heart of town and summoning every rat would rightfully terrify the citizens who took the effort to warn people about the danger. The warning to stay away was equally for them as it was for us. Being isolated meant they could handle the waves of an outbreak.

To that end, Warren and I rowed ourselves to shore in a small boat. A port that was capable of handling several large ships sat empty of all vessels and hands. It was clear that this part of town had been shut down for a while, but I couldn't tell if the rest of Hamelin was equally abandoned. Warren started to tie the boat against the dock while I grimaced at the barnacles on the piling along the waterline.

"You shouldn't rely on me or my magic to get you out of trouble with the Captain." Warren must have also been considering the warnings the town's people left.

I glanced over, wishing he'd mind his own business. "Yes, I know, Dread Pirate Bellamy. The entire crew is aware of your performances with the Captain."

Warren's steps came to a sudden stop as he flushed with embarrassment. I paused, surprised. I had not realized it was something he was bashful about, figuring it had been a game between the two of them. Possibly even aimed to be an aspirational sex life for everyone within earshot. Or maybe Warren was slightly prudish when not in the heat of passion.

He cleared his throat. "You know my last name?"

Or maybe that. "Is it outdated? I remembered it from the Queen's 'summer camp' for magical youth. I didn't recognize you until after I saw you do some wicked powerful magic during the last storm. Your appearance has altered a lot over the years, but your eyes remain the same."

After my explanation, Warren looked somehow more distant than when we started this conversation. "They change color?" I prompted. Only two people that I know of have a mismatched pair. And Warren's only changed when casting a strong healing spell.

"Yes, I know," Warren said harshly before he took a

centering breath. "Why don't I remember you?"

"Wasn't fucking memorable," I grumbled.

He shook his head in an instant. "That's not it. You're the most charismatically friendly man I've known."

I shrugged. That was the truth, but I wanted him to drop the topic so I could focus on the rat problem without actually needing to find a nest. If they truly were just rodents, I'd be able to play a song that spoke to them. Everything had an exact tune that spoke to it – if I spent enough time around it.

"Your cussing," Warren said with a laugh. "The Queen claimed swear words were as crass as actual curses."

"Such bullshit." I spat down at the dirt, knowing she was buried somewhere. "Screw her."

Warren laughed again, somehow making me smile as well when I glanced over. I appreciated how he left out that my youthful refusal to use 'proper language' got me singled out from the others as if my mouth carried an infectious plague of its own. There wasn't even much of a story besides me getting detention out in the harsh wind.

"What did she know about magic, anyway?" I ran a rough hand under my nose, trying not to think back. The thoughts lingered all the same. "Are you still friends with that one girl, Claudia? Once you got picked for the Queen's court, I stopped seeing her. Thought maybe she went with you?"

Warren shook his head. "She ran away."

"I should have done that." A mage school under the Queen's rule was a joke. She didn't teach; she tormented until something wondrous sprang out of you. In her eyes, I was a failure since my mouth was always quicker than my magic.

"She had help... I think," Warren continued, voice distant as if almost talking to himself. "Never could find her again to ask."

"Maybe one of the rats knows," I said in an attempt to get back to the job at hand.

This confession hour had not been my plan, so I focused on the thing that made me, well... me. And that was being a piper. This spot was as good as any. Near enough to the city that any rats shouldn't need long to reach us. But not so close, that we'd get the townspeople's attention first.

I lifted the pipe to my lips and played a tune that I would call all the rats in the city towards me. It was a lively song that I wrote for an audience of other shunned things.

I could hear the skittering background scratching before the first rat appeared. Dozens more came forth in several groups as the verses continued. There was probably one rat for each person within the town, and they gathered before us as I stopped playing.

Warren didn't back off from the possibly plague-infested animals. He did look alarmed over their sheer number but not afraid. Rats were outcasts too so they never bothered me, especially with a magical medic as backup.

"How'd you summon the trust of a whole species?" he asked.

"Could we drop our tragic backstories? We got a job to do, and I just did my share of it."

"Right, sorry." Warren stepped forward, hand outstretched as if able to sense something that I couldn't. "There's some disease here. But... It's not the rats that are the source of the danger. It's the fleas."

"Can you kill them off and heal any rodents that need

it?"

"I–yes." Warren's magic was softer sounding than most living things. He didn't need to play anything to cast, but I still could hear a whisper of notes in the wind. The less showy nature of his magic made me unsure of when he finished.

A rat scampered forwards toward us as if to offer thanks. Hopefully it was healthy. I glanced over to Warren, and he nodded that it was okay. I bent down to greet the animal and held my fingers out. The small rat climbed up and positioned himself perfectly in my palm.

"Guess animals just like me," I mused.

Warren smiled softly. There was a beauty and understanding there that made me jealous that he was with someone while I was on my own. But, unlike his now-false claim, I could never fall for any sea-loving pirate.

"I should get back to the ship," Warren said.

"You don't want to claim the reward with me? Surely 5% is yours."

Warren shook his head. We both knew that wasn't how the take was split on the ship. "I already have everything I want."

"I'll return later," I said and stood up. "The rest of those damn pirates will still want their share."

"Uh-huh," Warren added with no enthusiasm in his words. His hand touched my shoulder on his way back. "As long as you don't become a stranger."

CHAPTER TWO
- FINCH -

Hamelin had always been voted as the Best Port City in all Wonderland. I assumed it still would be if we acted like a coast was nearby. Now all trade was local, and the flow of visitors had cut back to next to no one. I was the Mayor four years ago when tourists first brought the plague to our city. It ravaged the young and old alike and left behind a very superstitious fear of rats. Since then, homes have been sealed up of any holes, and trees have been trimmed back to prevent them from crawling over rooftops. Debris, clutter, and garbage were taken out of town daily.

The vermin weren't abhorrently large or unusual in any real way, but even the sight of one was taken as an omen of death. Completely ridding the city of them had been the one campaign promise that I haven't ever been able to keep. That was why my campaign manager, Lana, was partially stressed going into tonight's meet and greet at the local tavern.

"Everyone's life is measurably better now," I said as she fussed over my hair. "Surely the least important thing won't be everyone's focus." Universal income had been a cakewalk faced with the logistics of getting the rats to leave. And the measures we took to lessen their population have brought several quality of life improvements already.

"How is that?" Lane said, ignoring my words and

holding up a handheld mirror.

The best part of her personality was that she didn't fight anyone over what they believed or did. She simply polished them up to best suit their natural traits. This was why she had slicked my hair back tonight; I had a nervous habit of running my hand through it. After a test, fussing with my hair now left the strands to flow in the same direction. I felt fresh and perfect for the re-election run to re-establish the people's faith in me. I was good at my job, but I wanted to make sure the people didn't think I was becoming complacent or incompetent.

We made it to the tavern in good time: just before it was naturally busy, and not so early that it looked like we had nothing better to do. Wooden stools sat against the high counter as the patrons in them leaned into the bartender. Alcohol prohibition was law, and its detractors had claimed that it would ruin the vibrance of this place. But, putting collective health first resulted in everyone being happier and free to spend time with each other.

The click of glasses full of sparkling cider or non-alcoholic beer overlapped over conversations. I smiled as we moved through the room, greeting everyone in passing. A larger man broke off from his existing conversations and stepped over to Lana and I. He'd been a dock worker years ago, but retirement had been treating him well. Still, I never fully trusted how well he was doing given his job didn't exist right now.

"I have never met a politician like you," he declared with a finger pointed at me. "You kept every promise. It's remarkable!"

"Pardon?" I asked.

He turned his broad chest to the rest of the tavern, holding his arms out boisterously. "Our hero, the once and future Mayor of Hamelin! Rat catcher extraordinaire!"

Lana politely clapped along to the crowd's cheers. I nervously ran my hand through my hair as Lana leaned into me to whisper. "Go along with this."

"You saw it," the man said, gesturing over to the bartender. She nodded back as she cleaned a glass. "Even I was worried when rats came down the street. Thought my end was nigh. Then watched as they drove themselves out of town."

"We will give you all the details later today!" Lana added, and the celebration got loud enough that she had enough cover to whisper to me again. "I'll go figure it out."

With that, she excused herself. I smiled and shook hands as people treated me like I had already won my re-election campaign, pretty sure my hairstyle considerations were utterly for naught now. *What was going on?*

Shortly after, a bright new color in the corner of my eye caught my attention. I focused in on the wearer's movements as a man stepped into the tavern. His outfit was a plethora of colors that he somehow pulled off with sheer confidence. Lana walked in after and gestured to him. The man was tall with a slight build and dazzling smile. His golden blonde hair lit up the room, and his piercing green eyes made me want to catch them simply for a closer look. I went white, realizing the most attractive man I've ever seen had wordlessly solved what I hadn't been ever able to.

"Everyone!" Lana called, taking the remaining focus off me. "Please welcome the Pied Piper of Hamelin! Our hero!"

Either his steps were soundless on the wooden floors or everyone's mirth had drowned out my hearing and rendered him ethereal. He looked out of place and breathtaking, like a rare bird sighting that was thought to be a myth. The world hushed as he came closer, and I believed everyone might be waiting along with me with a bated breath.

Lana brought him over to me. His eyes wide in amazement at everyone's reaction, shifted to pin me in place as he glanced over me from head to toe. As his lips quirked up into a smile, I felt like the only person in the room. Stars, his looks held up under close inspection.

I swallowed roughly and cleared my throat to speak. "Thank you. Our city and I are in your debt."

The piper's teeth caught his bottom lip before he replied in a breathy tone. "You have no idea."

I glanced over to Lana and was very glad that it would be impossible to make any drunken mistakes with him tonight. She must have noticed the spark between us too because she snapped into action like an overzealous chaperon about to call for a hand-check. With another promise about details later, she quickly whisked us outside. Well, as fast as I was allowed to leave any room—which was oftentimes very, very slow.

What I had failed to account for with her rescue was that when we all stepped out of the tavern, she went back inside. With nothing more than a comment about polling how everyone felt about the details, I was left to "sort the rest out."

"Lana, wait!" My plea went unheeded, and I had to remind myself I wasn't a horny teenager who needed supervision. In fact, I was an adult in charge of important goings-on because I enjoyed numbers, planning, and city management. I slowly turned from the closed door to face the handsome stranger. "Hello. Pleasure to meet you."

"Hi." The piper seemed to delight in my word choice with a soft laugh. He was either a little mad or maybe he also found me attractive—actually, he probably was just a little mad. What sort of rat-catcher wore a get-up like his? He must've been a mage. That would explain things. "Is your specialty summoning, sir?"

"Beauty and brains," the piper said playfully. "No wonder you're the biggest man in town."

His words did something for me, serving as another reminder that Lana had tasked me to get this situation under control. "What's your name?"

"Piper."

My eyes narrowed, and I nodded down at his belt and to the hand-stitched case he had made for his musical instrument. I would have brought up my concern regarding the title as a name, but I was certain he would turn the topic into an innuendo. "Right, sure."

Piper leaned against the alley's brick sidewall. "What's yours, O' Great Mayor of Hamelin?"

"Finch."

Piper smirked to himself. Oh, I wanted to kiss that cocky look off his face—I could kick myself for my lack of focus. "Did your parents think you'd be obsessed with birds?"

Nevermind... "A finch landed outside my mother's window when I was born. That's how I got my name."

"And yet you doubt mine," he countered. "Look, call me Snow White for all I care—"

"We should discuss business." My words were an accidental interruption as he finished his original thought.

"About the payment."

Shit, maybe I should have stalled and flirted back. "The office is closed," I countered. "You'll have to come back tomorrow morning. To fill out the needed paperwork and… whatnot."

Piper pushed himself off the wall, coming close enough to share the same air as I held my ground. "Can't we sneak in now?"

"No." It was hard to focus with him so close. He still smelled of the ocean and the long-forgotten vacations I used to take along the coast. Wait, what was I saying no about? "I'd have to gather the needed staff. Surely, you wouldn't summon an old lady from her bed simply because you refused to wait?"

"No?" Piper seemed to ask. And suddenly we were just two men who found themselves all too naturally in each other's personal space. Our voices were low, yet captivating. "Just what type of man are you, Mayor?"

"A good one," I said, all desire and defense as I remembered the dangerous quest he finished to even end up in our quiet town. "You perilous pied piper."

He waited as if I was about to prove my words or take something. I wasn't sure, so I moved a half step back. It was enough distance that I could turn back to go inside and not ditch my meet and greet.

"Finch!" Piper called.

I paused to hear him out, hand still on the tavern's door.

"Let's get one thing clear: I'm not your town's savior. I'm your town's newest hire."

I nodded back. No, he wasn't either of those things. He'd be my ruin if I wasn't careful.

CHAPTER THREE
- FINCH -

The next morning, I woke up clear-headed and ready to get as much work down as possible before Lana took me out on the single-city campaign circuit. The weather was as fair as could be while I walked over to Town Hall. I assured myself it would be a nice, normal, and easy day.

That thought lasted until I pulled open the door and saw Piper sitting on my receptionist's desk. Ms. Whitefall always got here before me to open up, and it seemed Piper was an equally early riser. His colorful outfit made him look so much like a delivery of flowers that I expected to find a note pinned to his shirt.

"Hello, Mayor Finch," Piper said with a wide grin. "Bean missing you."

Was there anyone who adored a pun as much as a mage? The ones I had come across always found humor where I could not. I forced a smile and managed to relax slightly after I glanced over at Ms. Whitefall, who at the very least, seemed alright with this situation. So far.

Piper sat up properly and crossed his legs that hung off the side of the desk. "I was hoping to espresso some strong opinions with you today."

Okay, he was clearly doing that on purpose. Wordlessly, we stared at each other for a moment before

Piper erupted into a laugh and turned to Ms. Whitefall, who gave him a tight smile back.

"He truly is bad at taking a hint," Piper said to her, eyeing me over again.

Oh. "You want me to go get you coffee?"

"You are already here." Piper glanced at Ms. Whitefall as if to direct my question to her. She gave a knowing look back, and Piper grinned again at me. "Bring some for us tomorrow morning."

Stars, help me if he was still here tomorrow.

Ms. Whitefall was a staple of the community. She'd been married for over fifty years and held this job before she even met her late husband. She was used to her bosses changing with each passing election, so she never let me be too personable with her. Which was why it was such a shock when she said, "You'll come to my birthday party this weekend?"

Even more stunning was that she meant the question for Piper. I'd been trying to get an invitation for weeks, even asking Lana for help. I wanted Ms. Whitefall to like me. Not just as a boss, but as a coworker. A person. Yet, Piper just walked here and did what I failed at within a single morning? Again?

"Of course," Piper said. "Seventy-five years deserves quite the celebration."

What in the stars was happening today? I cleared my throat before they unionized against me and my apparent cluelessness. "If you'll excuse us, Ms. Whitefall. Piper and I have some business to discuss."

I started walking to my office, and I heard Piper get up and follow behind me. For their apparent new friendship, it seems my receptionist still did her job dutifully and hadn't allowed Piper to go past her desk. Her attention didn't follow us either as I sat down at my desk.

He was a riot of color that I couldn't fully pull my attention away from, and he also seemed drawn to the only color in the office. Piper moved toward an indoor flowering plant by the window, and I was up in an instant, brushing his hands away from it. Mint was an easy plant to care for, but my window got too much sun in the afternoon, making it a temperamental thing. I've had to carefully bring it back from the brink of death twice already after a visitor's fussing attempted to liberate it from my office to the lobby where it got no direct sunlight.

My silent warning was met like the start of a dance. Piper's hands floated over to grasp mine and lift them between us. His thumb rubbed over my knuckles as I was caught off guard. He gave me a second to catch my bearing, but I failed before he started speaking.

"Kindly get your shit together and pay me already." His tone was too soft for the words coming out of his mouth, and I pulled my hands free.

I moved back to my desk and stared at the space between us with a new value and respect for the distance. "It will take a while for me to withdraw such a large sum from the bank. Surely, you'll be leaving again soon?"

Piper moved to sit in the chair in front of my desk. Kicking his feet up to rest at the corner. "It's fine. Ms. Lorance said I can stay as long as I need."

He knew Ms. Lorance too? Shit, why did I ever take my eyes off him? Piper's relaxed ease seemed to grow as every muscle of mine tensed. "The inn is closed to short-term visitors," I said stiffly.

"You'll find that money makes it easy to get what you want," Piper replied, leaning in as if telling me something I didn't exactly know. "Especially as this town's hero, the famed Pied Piper of Hamelin."

I needed to have a talk with Lana. There was movement at the door, and I hoped it was her. Instead, I found the masonry guild's representative in the doorway.

"Mayor Finch," the man said, extending his hand to shake.

I quickly rose to my feet and crossed the room to shake his calloused hand back. "Good morning, Mr. Hayes. If you'd excuse me and the piper for a moment?"

Mr. Hayes turned to Piper as if not even seeing him in the chair. Piper smiled politely as his manners caught up to him, and he took his feet off my desk. Before the mage could charm him, I grabbed Piper's arm and pulled him out of my office towards an empty conference room.

He blessedly held his tongue until we were alone again. "Buy a man a drink before leading him off somewhere next time."

It was clearly a joke, but I couldn't find it funny right now. Piper's amused expression didn't seem to care either way.

"Look," I said and took a deep breath. "How do I even know you got rid of the rat problem, as you claim?"

"Truly? Well, I can prove it with my friend."

Piper pulled the instrument off his belt, and my curiosity kept me silent as he played a beautiful little tune. Ms. Whitefall's yell pierces the silence left after his performance. I moved towards the door to check on her and spot a rat dashing inside. It quickly trotted over to Piper like a pet. Without fear, he lifted it in his hand as if to show me.

"I think I'll call him Warren. No, that could be confusing. Bell. Yes, that's a good name. Mayor Finch, this is my friend Bell. Would you like us to do a trick?"

What was wrong with this guy? "Piper, you can't just bring a rat to Town Hall."

Piper looked down at the oddly well-behaved creature in his hands. "Why not? He's friendly, healthy, and the proof you requested to see regarding my claim."

"I wanted every rat out of town."

"Fine." Piper set the rat down on the conference table and reached for his pipe again.

I grabbed his hand before he could play a single note. "You've proved your point. Please stop scaring my staff and take... Bell outside discreetly."

"We aren't finished talking."

I was going to be late for my meeting, and a rat was staring at me with beady little eyes that I didn't trust. "We can finish this later."

"When?"

"Lunch," I said, offering the only free time I could think of just so he would leave right now.

Piper held his hand out for the rat, and it crawled into his hand. "Is there a back door so I don't alarm the elderly amongst you?"

"Staff exit is at the end of the hall."

I watched him go with the shake of my head and then return to my office for back-to-back meetings, which proved far worse than I was expecting. Lana explained that Piper's actions have caused a record high for my approval rating. I rubbed at my temples, needing food or maybe even caffeine before this headache set in.

"What's the matter?" Lana asked, knowing me too well and sensing I was holding back. "You haven't upset him, have you?"

"No. Piper seems perfectly amicable."

"Good, keep it that way."

I had thought about lunch all morning. Not for the food, but about the man I promised to catch up with during it. Maybe I should tell her about my money-related concerns. If anyone could think of a way out of this, it was her. But I was afraid she would find me a lost cause if I did.

"Certainly. If you'll excuse me?"

Lana nodded and commented that we'd discuss things more after my last meeting at the end of the day. I expected to have a moment for myself as I left out the back door, but Piper was sitting on the ground across from the door, waiting for me.

I glanced around the alleyway, not seeing his pet rat or anything that would entertain him. If I'd known he wouldn't have gone far, I would have at least offered a chair inside. "Have you been out here the whole time?"

Piper looked up at me, making no indication he was ready to move. "Sent the rat past the outskirts of town first."

"Do you know where that even is?"

"No, but Bell certainly did."

At a loss for how a rat could not only know but respect the wish made me frown. Piper continued to watch before he mirrored my expression, rising to his feet and looking like making me unhappy was his only regret of the day. There were footsteps to our right, and before I glanced toward the sound, Piper pulled me back into the shadows along with him.

It was almost midday, and there was just enough cover for us to stand. I noticed the temperature difference being just out of the direct sun and Piper's hands lingering on my arms even after his direction to move closer.

"No one is coming this way," I quipped, flattered that he seemed to want to keep me for himself.

"How was I to know that?" A flush crept across his face before he inhaled, chest rising as his confidence ebbed back.

My heart was pounding over his possessive little act. Given the fact that I was the one who didn't have their back flush to the wall, it was particularly tempting, as if granting me equal footing. "You're dangerous."

"Some have even called me perilous," he teased, as his head turned towards the people who moved further away from us.

A somber smile tugged across my face as I remembered my words from yesterday. No one besides my staff would ever come or go this way, so I knew we would have a moment. As if in a dream, my hand raised cautiously into his remaining space, turning his chin towards me so I owned his full attention at this moment.

His hand snaked up to rest behind my neck and pulled me down into a kiss. His lips were lush as they parted between mine. With a shiver, goosebumps prickled down my arms. His tongue rolled over my lower lip, and I felt like I was going to lose my mind.

Piper exhaled a ragged breath, swaying forward towards me as I broke us apart. I watched silently as his eyes seemed to focus on where he was instead of just who he was with.

Wait, who was I with? I couldn't help but suddenly wonder if he needed such a large sum of money. Would he bring trouble to town if I didn't pay fast enough? "Are you an honest man, Piper?"

"I…" He shook his head and studied my face. "I don't know what you're exactly asking."

With a glance over my shoulder, I reassured myself that there was still time to discuss this. "Do you always tell the truth?"

"Aye, what's the fun of playing the game if we aren't honest?"

I took a step back and adjusted my clothes as if he had ruffled them. Clearing my throat, I swallow down the massive lie I started us out on. The truth was… an easily hidden thing.

There was no money to pay him. During the height of the plague, I had given the town every last thing I owned to keep everyone housed and as happy as they could be. I knew I'd be fine with my free housing and a purpose as mayor, but I wouldn't even take my pay until next year. Even if I gave Piper every cent of that, I'd still need much more.

"Let's get some lunch," I said. I needed another moment or two to figure out what I wanted, what was owed to him, and how to offset the risk of each.

CHAPTER FOUR
- PIPER -

This early in the morning, the only heated discussions outside of Town Hall were the calls of birds that quibbled over the rising morning sun. Ms. Whitefall's pace was casual and slow as I watched her approach. She was very friendly but a stickler for the rules. Even if she broke into a sprint, nothing would have opened the door before the sundial outside declared it open to the public.

"Morning, madam," I said and rose off the front steps.

"Good morning."

I waited until she unlocked the door and then held it open for her like a true gent. Just like the day before, I sat on the corner of her desk as she began her work. Finch was actually the third in today, only beaten by Lana who sped by fast with a quick greeting to us both.

The mayor stopped short, hands still lingering on the door handle as he looked me over with wide eyes. There was always a curiously apprehensive study of all my colors, as if his eyes needed a moment to adjust. It was a gaze I returned with more certainty as I noted that there was no coffee in his hands.

Like his campaign manager before him, he quickly picked up the pace and gave us both a passing hello. Ms. Whitefall shook her head to herself once he was down the hall.

"Shall I go get us coffee?" I asked and pushed myself off the desk.

"You don't need to do that, dear."

"Course not, but what else am I going to do today?"

The tavern I was first brought to wasn't far. While not exactly a cafe, I hadn't seen a more suitable place to get coffee. The door had been open when I passed this morning, so they must serve breakfast of some sort.

The city was more alive than the pier. It seemed they just lived their lives away from the lands and learned they didn't need the commerce to be self-sustaining between themselves. There were a few people inside the tavern, including a family which seemed out of place.

The bartender nodded an acknowledgment as she wiped down the counter in front of her. I took a seat at the spot she just cleaned. "Do you serve coffee?"

"We do." The woman smiled. "Just the one?"

"Two please."

She smirked but said nothing as she went to brew the cups.

I wasn't sure who she thought the other was for, but I didn't want the truth to cause a stir if Mr. Whitehall was still around. Instead, I looked at the back wall where one would see the top-shelf liquor. There were bottles, but they were empty—possibly even dusty.

"Do you not serve booze?"

"It's a dry town," she said, sitting down two cups before glancing up towards the bottles. "Haven't been able to pour any since the plague. The night before the prohibition, everyone finished all of those bottles. Now, if people come in complaining they want something, I just remind them of the wicked hangovers they all got. Wild discard for moderation that night." Her story ended with a laugh, and I smiled along.

"Is that the Mayor's doing?"

"Nah. Well, more of a compromise." She leaned into the counter, voice dropping lower. "What do you think of him?"

I sat up at the direct question. "Finch?"

She nodded, but her serious look made me think she was asking for a review of how good his lips tasted. "Treating you well? Sometimes I worry that without tourists we'll fall behind the rest of the lands."

"The no booze thing seems old-fashioned. But otherwise…" I said before I lost the forcefulness needed to explain how not great things had been since the disappearance of the King. He'd been a lost boy turned royal, a symbol of change that did not last long. "Look, this place seems nice. I've been traveling around for a while now doing odd jobs. And no one here seems to do anything they don't want. That's freedom."

"Besides the booze."

"Besides the booze." I grinned at her and picked up the mugs. "What do I owe you?"

"Coffee's free."

"See? Wonderful place you have here."

Thankful that I didn't need to search my pockets for coins, I headed back to Town Hall before the coffee had even fully cooled. Placing one down on Ms. Whitefall's desk, I was rewarded with a wide smile for my efforts.

I didn't think Finch was actively trying to ignore his staff's wants; more so, it was the lack of words being said that caused the miscommunication. She just seemed stubborn in her ways, while the Mayor might be a hair away from being overwhelmed.

As I drank my coffee, I glanced down the hall, trying to peek into his office. The memory of his kiss yesterday returned, and I might have added pink to the overall look I had going today.

"Do you fancy him?" Ms. Whitefall asked, grinning like she was a witness to an opening night of a new play.

"Just trying to figure out when he's actually going to pay me for ridding the town of pests."

"Vile things, those rats." Ms. Whitefall added, before leaning in like she had a secret to tell me. "I wouldn't hold my breath. He's a bad tipper."

"Tipping culture is vile." The reply wasn't meant as an insult, but she pursed her lips together like I'd been crude. Must be a generational gap between us. "Wages shouldn't be selectively gifted. Imagine those who'd suffer under poor gifters."

"That must explain it," Ms. Whitefall said. "Mayor Finch is rubbish at gifts. That's why I didn't invite him to my birthday."

I grinned, sprawling out with my lean even further over her desk. "Let me go see if I can shake something loose."

"Shake a leg."

I found the Mayor where and doing what you'd expect. His eyes pulled up to me only briefly as I walked in and took a seat. But just as quickly, he went back to what he had been doing—which seemed to be writing. Maybe a new stump speech, since that whole rat problem wasn't an issue anymore.

His quill started to run out of pigment, and instead of

dipping it into the inkwell, he licked the tip before attempting the word again. Finch didn't seem to get much further than a few letters before needing to dip it into a small bottle with grayish ink. The speech writing was smooth sailing for a short while before he ran out of space on the page. Instead of grabbing a fresh sheet, he searched his desk for a suitable piece of paper to reuse and flipped it over to the back to continue.

"You aren't a bad tipper or shit gifter. You're fucking poor."

Finch sucked air through his front teeth. It was enough of a reaction that I knew he'd heard some part of my theory before. Whatever thought he'd been jotting down was likely lost as he stared up at me. "Wherever did you hear that?"

"Who do you think?" I mused, delighted with his focused worry.

His hand pulled up to his lips, measuring his response carefully. "Is it meant to be obvious?"

"Come on, Finch." I leaned back in the seat, but he seemed unwilling to budge from his position. "Are you only going to answer my question with another so you can toe the line of you not becoming a liar?"

Finch's expression fought back what surely had to be another question of some sort. "No."

"You owe me a lot of money."

His serious eyes glanced away from mine. "I know."

"You need to figure it out before it's figured out for you."

I pushed up from my seat and headed down a hall that started to feel all too familiar. There didn't seem to be footsteps following behind me, but I heard my name called before I reached the exit.

He didn't continue, so I turned around with a sigh and found him nervously wringing his hands. Finch shifted on his feet, and I nearly saw the gears turn as he tried to do what he'd promised. "I'll see you tomorrow?"

A small part of me wanted to show him mercy. "Bet on it."

CHAPTER FIVE
- FINCH -

There was distant music playing as I walked into Town Hall. Just four notes cut through the near morning silence and finished as I stepped inside the building. The wind shifted, pushing the door closed behind me with enough force that both Ms. Whitefall and I glanced at its strange behavior.

Bird calls chimed melodically before shouts from outside covered their songs up. I opened the nearest window to learn more and spotted a black swarm twisting down the street in midair. As they neared, the details became clearer to reveal a flock of birds.

I jumped out of the way as Lana stepped into the office at an inopportune time. The birds casually landed without regard to the surface as long as it was flat enough. We both froze, stunned since it was something out of a... well, a *fairytale*.

Ms. Whitefall yelped as a bird hopped on her desk. "This filthy thing is going to poo over my papers!"

Okay, maybe more of a *nightmare* depending on your opinion of birds.

The same song from before was repeated as Piper walked into the room. He stopped playing once all eyes were on him. "Good morning, public servants of

Hamelin."

"Just what are you doing?" Lana asked, her usual neutral tone slipping.

"Simply wanted to gather every bird in your fine city together to show support for the re-election for their *Mayor Finch*." His sing-song and dance ended with a glance towards me, and I had to cover my mouth to keep from laughing.

"How…" Lana eyed the birds for a moment, maybe considering the production value of dove releases and similar displays. "Charming."

I needed to quickly build a bridge, so this didn't end in an argument over tactics. "Yes, he's a regular prince," I said and waved him closer to me so we can talk.

Like magic, he stepped over, unobstructed as the rest of my staff remained jumpy over any sudden flutter. We moved down the hall for a further buffer. These birds were hardly rats with wings, but I understood their worry even if I didn't share it. Piper was clearly in control.

"You must be extremely proficient with magic to summon multiple types of animals with such precision," I said, more impressed than anything else.

"It's just practice," Piper answered, with a roll of his eyes. "Everyone sees a mage and thinks they are just born able to do whatever they desire. No one stops to think about the effort or damage it took first."

"Oh, Piper." His name fell from my mouth with such softness that I didn't even think he heard it. The rest of the staff definitely didn't, their attention still focused on countless birds flitting around the office, unable to settle since they couldn't either.

I was tempted to reach out to him. No one else would notice. But I needed to de-escalate this first, so I cleared my throat loudly above all the noise to signal *I* was the boss. "What is your endgame here?"

Piper seemed to mull over the answer as if it was the first time he'd given it thought. "I don't know. Lure you into a life of crime? Laugh when you lose your re-election to a dog?" He grinned again.

"Very cute." My teeth clenched at the very thought. "No dogs are running for mayor."

A bird landed on his shoulder, and I hoped it would whisper something divinely good on my behalf. His sharp green eyes found me again and held a playful chaos. I couldn't convince myself malice existed too, even as he taunted me.

"That's why it would be so funny when one bests you."

"There's actually no one running against me." Piper's eyes widened, light sparkling there over my words and the critical mistake I just made. Lana would kill me if he ran for Mayor against me. The thing about politics was someone didn't need to mean harm to ruin your career. "I'm begging you, please... *don't*. If I lose, there'll be no way to pay you."

Piper turned to the bird, shrugging a single shoulder just enough to signal to the bird it should move. "You have until I tire of these games."

Lana stepped over to us and ducked away from the bird as it flew away. "Gracious, Piper. You certainly have proved your skills to everyone here."

"But?" Piper prompted with a wide grin.

She pulled her hands together with a clap that looked like she was about to pray. Lana loathed leading questions. It gave me solace Piper delighted in teasing anyone. "But," she conceded, "it would be troublesome if the people thought the lack of rats caused an invasion of birds."

"Only meant to show my support for the Mayor here," Piper said, all smiles even as mine wavered. It was hard to deny he enjoyed tormenting me the most.

"How lovely of an endorsement," Lana continued. "Perhaps next time you could use your words, rather than songs?"

"Perhaps." Piper leaned in as if to bow before excusing himself, quite literally playing himself out as the birds followed him behind flying free once outside.

I couldn't tell why I was disappointed that Piper didn't turn back up the next day. The day dragged until lunch, and I couldn't deny that my mind slowed, unable to take in the words I had been reviewing. I wandered out into the lobby only to find Ms. Whitefall there. Her birthday was yesterday, so she might have been the last person to have seen that damn Piper. That was if he was even allowed to join the celebrations after his little show.

Not wanting to directly ask, I went vague and focused on the party itself. My poll numbers have been up since the rats left town, so I shouldn't have been worried about what she and Piper thought about me. And yet, it was all that mattered.

Ms. Whitefall seemed to know what I was trying to do, and she was not falling for it. "Gossip must never be shared with the boss about private events." She moved her hands under the desk, and I wondered if I missed any new jewelry on her wrist.

"Right you are, Ms. Whitefall." I couldn't fault her for keeping the boundaries she wanted between her work and home life. But we shared an office, and it was around noon. "May I go get you lunch?"

Her eyes narrowed and highlighted her winkles. "That would be nice."

I left and shortly returned with the standard free lunch from the tavern. I didn't expect it to improve her mood at all given it was one of the three things always offered. But she smiled up at me as I placed it on my desk.

Wait. Did she not like walking over to the tavern? Age had slowed her down, but I never asked how much. Would that explain why even though she *could* grab herself coffee in the morning, and did usually get lunch herself, she found it nicer if I did it on her behalf? *Was it her pride or mine that caused the miscommunication?*

She must have seen the question on my face and laughed to herself. "You know," Ms. Whitefall started as she poured dressing onto her salad. "That pied piper is good for you."

"For the whole town, apparently," I retorted.

Maybe he *would* be elected mayor instead of me. Or maybe he'd just convince no one to vote, and I'd lose by default. Without a word, I headed to my office to eat alone.

As I searched my drawers for a fork to eat with, I found a caramel apple sitting on a napkin. A bakery on the other side of town made these. I recognized the delicious sheen the candy coating gave it. Even if I had found utensils, my salad was lackluster in comparison. I lifted the apple as if within a fairytale for the second day. I bit in, and the smell and texture made my eyes water. I coughed out the bite back onto the napkin unceremoniously. The apple looked strange, and the scent completely gave it away what it was: *an onion.*

Tickled that I hadn't been poisoned, I busted into laughter against the coughing fit. That damn Piper didn't even show up today to see the result of his prank this time. We'd need to talk if I ever wanted a normal workday again.

I went to the only place I thought made sense for him to be and soon greeted the innkeeper, Ms. Lorance. The front office was empty of people and acted as more of a living space now than a place of work. Ms. Lorance was at her desk with a worn book in hand.

"Good day. Is that pied piper around?"

"Oh yes," she said and quickly grabbed a bookmark. "He's rented out the large room. Was that all you needed, Mayor Finch?"

"Yes, thank you."

She smiled and returned to her book. I knew where the suite was. There'd been a big political hoopla over a few years back. Three of the smaller rooms were given semi-permanently to people who needed housing. But the property had four small rooms and two larger rooms. Ms. Lorance never married or had kids, so there was a fight over who could get the remaining suite. I had suggested leaving it open for actual guests, along with the remaining small room.

The urge to ask how Piper afforded it, or if he was already borrowing against the debt I owed him, was on the top of my want list. But there simply was no way to ask that without Ms. Lorance finding out that Piper had yet to be paid.

Piper's room was quiet, candles lit despite daylight from a large window, and floors neatly swept. Likely Ms. Lorance's doing. Piper sat in a high-backed chair, adjusting his instrument. The *actual* pipe he played. Not that my mind didn't go elsewhere as I watched his confident fingers fiddle.

"I found your *apple*," I said, feeling like we were past the need for proper greetings. "Sweet of you to leave me a surprise."

He looked up at me through his lashes. "I heard an apple a day keeps the doctor away."

"Is that so?" I asked, stepping further into the room so I could close the door behind me and we wouldn't be overheard. "Then what does an onion do?"

I waited with bated breath as he put down the pipe and gave me his undivided attention. "Brought you to me."

"Is that what you want?" The question felt so dangerous once it left my lips. I had meant the comment innocently, but it didn't sound that way when I heard it back.

His expression smoldered, as if feeling the same heat between us. "You know what I want." *What a dangerously loaded answer.* "Give it to me."

Piper stood and walked over before I had the good sense to do anything besides have my eyes follow his path that ended in front of me.

Belatedly, I moved back and bumped into the door. "Give *what* to you?"

"What do you think?" His green eyes dilated, and his hand moved out of sight. I gasped in a rush of fear, then pleasure, as he grabbed my crotch in the moment between his words. "Hamelin's crown jewels?"

"Piper…" My words were a warning as much as an invitation.

"Not the P-word I was thinking about." His grin grew, and his wicked grip tightened without causing pain. His lips parted as if to guide mine to follow.

And I did mirror him with the overwhelming urge to

kiss him. It was all too much—I couldn't think with him this close.

A low laugh rumbled through Piper's chest as he answered his own question. "Payment."

"Didn't forget," I grumbled and brushed his hand away. "Or did *you* overlook your acute observation that the city is broke? Every coin is accounted for."

Piper nodded. He even backed off from me, giving me just enough personal space to collect my senses. "Yes, how *did* that happen? Did you embezzle it all for a fancier home?"

"*No!* Of course not. I spent the bounty fund on food services."

He blinked, confused like I'd done something unbelievable and unfathomable; magical, even. I've never seen a mage give someone without any magic that look. It was the type of thing shared between people who did what was considered impossible. A hushed, wowed, *huh*.

"What's the matter?"

Piper licked his lips and looked around the room. Maybe he was looking for an excuse or pause to allow an interruption. But it was just the two of us, so I waited for him to answer.

"You've failed to account for me."

CHAPTER SIX
- PIPER -

The fuck was I doing, playing around with a man like this? One that found me funny. And one I found equally hypnotic. The Mayor was a good man. I wanted to know every last thing he excelled at besides being a caring leader.

This was not how the game was meant to go. He was supposed to find me annoying and pay his bill quickly so I could move on to another town. Away from Hamelin, and far away from him.

"The city doesn't have the money to pay you," the Mayor seemed to remind me after I'd been standing there dazed.

"Well," I started and took my seat, crossing my legs to posture further. "I did a service for you and your fair city. Maybe it's time for *you* to pay up."

"*Me?*" He stammered, as if out of stock of the syllables needed to continue speaking.

"Find something."

Instead of deflating to the pressure, he rallied with a sarcastic attitude. "What do you want, the clothes off my back?"

What a curiously wonderful idea. I eyed the dapper waistcoat that sat under a tailored long-sleeved jacket as a smile crept over my face. "You do seem to value appearance. Take them off."

"What?"

"Take them off," I repeated. "Or is this yet another payment you refuse after offering?"

"I'm—This is outrageous."

The surprised objection in his voice was clear, so I didn't push further. I just waited in silence to see if he'd remember how close he was to the door and leave. Instead, the good Mayor marched over to the window that faced the bay and pulled the curtains closed. The light in the room dimmed, but what sneaked past mixed with the candles, leaving it still bright enough to see he made his choice.

There was another step towards me before he stopped short. Both hands grabbed at his jacket before he remembered how to disrobe.

"Slower."

Finch caught my gaze. I wasn't sure what he saw in me, but it was something that made him easily flush. As he rose to the challenge, the air between us grew heated.

"Like this?" Instead of casually pulling off the jacket and handing it to me, he was dragging an arm out of a sleeve, teasing me with hints of skin along his bicep and then wrist.

"Perfect."

With care, he laid his jacket down on the bed. "Maybe I can pay you another way."

I almost lost the shape of his words, too busy wondering if his mouth would taste of onion from my prank. Or if he plucked a mint leaf off the plant in his office and bitterly chewed it first. The pressure of my teeth on my lower lips slipped as I smiled wider. "And how's that?"

Finch took a breath like a diver before he stepped toe to toe with my shoes and sank to one knee. Soon, fully kneeled to keep better balance as his hands hovered without touching. "What's the saying? Put your money where your mouth is?"

"Not sure that's how..." I shook my head. Who cared what the rest of the saying was or what it was meant to mean? He made me excitedly anxious, and I would've rather not said a word if any could break us apart. I just uncrossed my legs to see what he planned to do next.

Finch's hands started at the hem of my pants, giving everything else very little attention, and undressing me *just* enough to give him the real estate he needs. My mind wandered to how I was meant to share 10% of *this* with the pirates. Maybe I would offer Finch a discount and lower it to only their share on account of good behavior.

As the thought went on, I realized Finch paused too. "What's wrong?"

"Nothing. It's just," he interrupted himself to clear his throat, "bigger than I expected."

I grinned to keep from outright laughing. What compelled him to finish his real thought out loud? *What a delightful man.*

He looked up at me from the ground, fingers idly running across sensitive skin. "You're enjoying this too much already."

"You are too, given the way my dick hasn't left your hand."

Finch flushed as his hold fluttered away as if he had not realized his actions. Afraid I may have painted him into a corner he didn't want to be in, I backpedaled. "We don't have—"

I lost my words to a gasp as the warmth of his mouth surrounded me. "*Fuck.* That's right, fucking take my cock." Saying crude words to such a proper man seemed to protect my sanity. A reminder that this wasn't anything besides physical.

My hips tilted up, reaching deeper into his mouth. And a moan echoed back, egging me on. Finch pulled up and away to add a long, teasing lick. "Am I the best you've ever had?"

"Actually," I said, "the best is yet to come." I aimed to joke, because, well, we'd both be insufferable with our egos inflated.

"Oh, shut the fuck up."

This time, I couldn't hold back my amusement. I was too giddy with enjoyment already, even as his mouth fully lifted off me in objection. "Wait! Come back, it was a joke."

"You're not funny," he insisted but didn't stand up.

"It's not funny," I replied, feeling far too agreeable. The Mayor aggressively took me back in his hand as if claiming it as his. "I'm only doing this so when I give you the best orgasm of your life, you remember who gave it to you and hate yourself for it."

"Uh-huh, big talk for someone—*mmm.*"

"Would you stop talking?" Finch mumbled against me, holding me back from finishing. There was no way he didn't know exactly what he was doing. He was enjoying himself by making this payback for my pranks.

"Please," I moaned. My hands moved down to the sides of his head with a gentle hold that showed I wanted him to stay between my legs. *"Please."*

His lips slid over my head, his tongue doing something I couldn't even process as I started twitching, whining, and coming so hard it startled me.

"You okay there?" Finch asked. I knew he was grinning ear to ear from the sound even though my eyes were closed as I enjoyed the waning bliss.

"Where did you learn to do that?" As I tilted my head back down, I caught him shrug.

"Dunno, just golden ruled it."

"Golden rule," I mocked. There was a trash pail within reach, and I stretched out of the chair to grab it and weakly pretended to throw up.

"You're so dramatic," he said, smile still lingering. "Would you leave already?"

"What, town? My dick isn't even back in my pants yet. Would you wait a damn second lest I break some indecency law?"

Finch watched me as if he was proud of how well he unraveled me while I laced my pants. Then he asked the most curious thing. "Would you like to come to dinner? There's another campaign event tonight."

"You haven't had enough of me yet?"

"Everyone in town adores you." When I didn't reply, Finch's head tilted. "We're good, right?"

"Yeah, we're good." I'm afraid to clarify what he means by *we*. As in his bill, we as two people, or some political pawn useful for re-election. "But isn't dessert usually saved for after dinner?"

He chuckled. "I won't tell anyone if you don't."

CHAPTER SEVEN
- FINCH -

Piper didn't show up for dinner. But he was sitting on my desk the following morning, and I felt like I won him from Ms. Whitefall. He wasn't doing anything besides killing time and humming to himself while I worked.

A bit later, I caught his hand gently batting at my plant. I hadn't planned on confronting Piper like *that* yesterday. And I was very glad Lana picked mint for my office because it came in handy.

"Leave my plant be. Why are you still here if you're bored?" To be honest, I liked having him around. He never asked me to sign or read anything, and he was colorful enough that my eyes readjusted simply with a glance.

Piper lifted a shoulder to barely commit to a shrug. "The pirates I sailed in with aren't at the harbor."

"Pirates?" If I had known he'd come in with a large ship, I would have demanded a more thorough quarantine. "They aren't still there, are they?"

"Don't you listen? I just told you they aren't," Piper scolded. "They probably won't be back until the new moon."

I grimaced at the idea of more people. Especially pirates that rarely followed any law aside from their own.

"Don't give me such a sour look unless you're going to confess you don't want me to leave."

"I'm sorry, it's just—"

Piper stood, and I caught his hand before he could pull away. I think it surprised us both how easily I had.

"I know," he said, "and I wouldn't put your people at risk. It was the ticks, by the way. Not the rats that spread the plague."

"How do you know that?" Our hands dropped from each other, but my steady gaze urged him to answer.

"A mage friend of mine; he's a healer. I brought him with me to get rid of the rats. Wherever they go, they won't bring death on their backs."

"A mage?" I asked, thinking back. "Is it the Warren you mentioned before?"

Piper's eyes caught the light as he smiled. "You do listen to me."

"I listen to all my constituents," I teased.

"Piper can't vote," Lana said as she walked into my office without so much as a courtesy knock. "And don't even suggest he can. Here's the guest list for tonight. Make sure you memorize everyone's plus-one or they'll think you don't care."

"Thank you, Lana." My voice carried my wariness as I stared down at the fresh papers. She gave me a lackluster *uh-huh* in reply.

"There's an annual masquerade ball tonight?" Piper asked, pulling the invite out from under the other papers my campaign manager brought. "I could take you."

His words were like a gift-wrapped grenade. I didn't know what I was meant to do with it, and knowing Piper, the danger might only be glitter. Either way, I needed to defuse the situation before it blew up. "Like, in a fight?"

Piper smirked. "Yeah, sure. That too."

I said nothing else as I glanced at Lana and saw the gears of thought turning. Her chin lifted after deciding. "Actually, why don't you join us? Plenty to celebrate now that you're in town."

Piper grinned down at the invite, looking so adorable I knew there wasn't anything besides having fun on his mind. "Okay, I'll go find some proper attire?"

I flushed, remembering his type of merriment.

"That sounds great," Lana said, sounding surprised. I think it amazed her that her plan didn't equate to any more added work.

After another smile over at us, Piper left my office.

Lana shook her head at the empty doorway. "I don't know what you did to make him adore you, but good job."

She patted me on the back, and I tensed at her touch. I definitely couldn't tell her how I figured out how to pay my debt. Taking my silence for a willingness to study, she made for the door.

"He doesn't adore me," I called after her.

"Uh-huh," she said, turning the corner.

"He came in with pirates!"

Lana leaned back in the doorway in a flash, hand on the frame like an anchor pulling her back. "*No*," she said, finger moving to point at me. "No one said or will be saying that. Hamelin's hero can't run off one fear, only to replace it with another."

She paced in front of my desk, considering the new information. "Make sure he follows the rules and keep him entertained. Can you do that?"

I nodded.

"Good." With a controlled exhale, she smiled down at the papers she brought. "And remember, the blacksmith's name is pronounced Row-*cheek*. Not check. Mind your accent."

After another nod, she left for real this time. I sighed into the empty room. I doubted names or guests would be a problem, unless it was my plus-one. Fooling around with Piper was a dangerous game that I should not be enjoying, let alone one that should be encouraged by people who didn't know the whole truth.

Piper stole any objection from me when I saw the outfit he showed up on my doorstep in.

"That good, aye?" He spun around to showcase his three-piece suit of all different shades of gold.

I've seen the fabric in the tailor's shop before, but I wouldn't have thought to put all of it together. Despite the ornate details on the clothes, it was his mask that I had trouble taking my eyes off of. Cut pieces of black leather were sewed together to make a wolf's ears and snout that extended past his face. The artistry even included hashes on the surface to suggest fur.

"May I come in?"

I shook my head both as a no and to shake off the spell I wanted to be pulled under. "No... uh, the ball's not here. It's at the Guild of Seamstress' ballroom."

"Oh," Piper said, rocking up on the balls of his feet. "Thought since you had the biggest house in town, the party would be here. Don't tell Lana I don't know where things are."

"I won't."

My attention lingered on his covered face as we walked. My mask didn't fit as well as his. It was an antique, originally molded for a face that was not mine. It was ornate and traditional for a masquerade. Almost like the manor I lived in. He, however... literally had teeth.

"It's not a costume party," I said.

"That would explain why you look dashing, but... I don't know." He glanced ahead, then dropped the topic.

Today was about people being entertained, and that included him. "Tell me."

"I only mean it's a party. It's meant to be fun," Piper said, then gestured from my chest to face. "So, what are you anyway?"

"The mayor." That was the original owner of my mask, and who it would go to when I was replaced—hopefully, many years from now.

"You're the mayor every day."

"And I intend to continue to be so."

Piper sighed. "Where's the fun in that?"

"I enjoy my job," I said.

"You're a bore."

Shit. I'd been specially told not to be boring. "Don't take your mask off," I said in a panic. The dance hall was steps away now, and we needed to be on the same page fast. "It's a statement piece. You'll be the only one with an extra set of ears. And fangs."

"Suppose that is fun," Piper said, before gesturing towards the door. "Shall I get it for you?"

Him deferring to me would be good optics. And since he was offering. "Yes, thank you."

"Don't mention it," he said and opened the door for himself. Then stepped inside, back to the door. His magnetic presence pulled everyone's attention to our way, and by the time I followed behind, it was like being given a royal announcement.

Lana snuck in a quick thumbs-up as we passed and mingled with the crowd. The upper echelon of our city changed fairly often with different union elections and personal relationships. The staples twirled around on the dance floor while nearly everyone else stayed at their assigned tables to appear respectful of where they were.

I was impressed by how undemanding Piper was as a plus-one. He never asked to dance, something I assumed would have been his favorite. Nor did he complain about the lack of drink in his hand. He helped me socialize and would almost, unconsciously, direct us towards the back of the room with the other musicians. Conversations didn't linger beyond their natural expiration, and no one group seemed to be ignored or overly favored.

"Mr. Rowcheek," I said, as the burly blacksmith stepped over to us from his table, purely out of obligation. That was clear because his plus-one stayed sitting at the table. Angela, I thought—not that it mattered since I couldn't properly greet her. "How are you doing tonight?"

"Quite well, Finch," he said, and I could smell the booze on his breath. Lana thought he never liked me because I didn't always annunciate as clearly as I should. The truth was I knew he made moonshine but couldn't say anything since he was the blacksmith's representative. While it wasn't legal, it was decriminalized so there's nothing to be done for the rule breaking.

He turned to Piper with more interest than he had for me. "I suppose you must've heard many stories about the new Wolf King in your travels given your flare tonight."

Piper nodded, seeming at a loss for words, as he must have picked up the scent as well. He stole a glance over at me before smiling. "Did you hear the tale about how the Wolf fell in love with a Robin?"

Mr. Rowcheek's laugh sounded like gravel. "How would that even be possible? Would the wolf open its maw and carefully hold the bird between its sharp teeth?"

That wasn't right in the slightest. I didn't think he was wasted, but he must've thought the Wolf King was an actual wolf rather than a man with one. Piper shot me an expecting look before his green eyes flicked back towards the blacksmith.

Oh, he was giving me a chance to agree with someone I usually couldn't.

"Pray tell, what's the moral there?" I asked.

Piper angled himself towards me. "Must all stories have one, Mayor Finch?"

I grinned. "Wouldn't have figured you'd be one for royals and fairytales."

"Didn't say I believed in them," Piper said, with a flirtatious amount of coyness.

Mr. Rowcheek grunted at Piper's answer. "If you'll excuse me, Mayor."

Stunned he called me by my title, I almost missed the chance to say goodbye. "Take care." My voice grew louder to account for the distance, and Angela looked up from the combination of movement and sound. "Say hello to your wife for me," I added with a wave.

That worked perfectly.

I turned to the musician. "How'd you do that?"

"Do what?" Piper asked, grinning. "That performance made me hungry."

I gestured over to the food table and was thankful my status made it so we did not have to wait to be served. My plate was largely for show since I never actually ate at these things. "You know, you could charm the pants off anyone."

Piper stuffed his face with food. "Why would I want anyone when you look so good in those pants?"

"Pardon?" My voice dipped low, embarrassed people would hear. "These are my normal pants."

"Don't I know it." He clicked his tongue before tipping an oyster into his mouth. It quickly slid back onto his plate, much like the onion he gave me. Except his tongue stayed hanging out, and I considered grabbing a waste bin. "So gross, too salty."

"What's wrong with you?" I laughed, feeling more like myself than I had all night. "Why did you grab one if you don't like them?"

"Never had one before."

I watched him, expecting more, but he said nothing else. Piper even paused to look up at me like I was being the odd one.

"Do you want to get out of here?" I found myself asking.

"Won't Lana be upset?" Piper's eyes darted over to where she was but no longer stood.

"We never checked our coats?"

"I don't know," Piper said, placing his plate down

before taking mine and setting it on top. "Are you stunningly handsome under that mask of yours?"

"Hush. At least until we are alone," I said, fearing I might kiss him in front of everyone if he kept flattering me. I supposed nothing said I couldn't here and now; I simply didn't want that to be the story of the night.

The coat check was just a large closet. Hopefully, it would remain empty of other people since it was the middle of the party. I would have been happy to sit and not talk for a moment, but Piper took the first opportunity he could to push my mask up and off my face.

"My stars, mister," Piper teased as he leaned in. The intensity of his focus was in every line of his body. I pulled him ever closer as he continued to speak. "You have a face for politics."

Did the Wolf King's eyes have such an endless depth of color? "Can I take your mask off?"

"You're the one who asked to keep it on," he countered, hand lifting to untie the string along the back. Maybe the King would have been easier to tame since I could barely handle Piper's force of will.

"You know I hate you, right?" Piper said. "I absolutely can't stand a hypocrite in power." His playful tone made it sound like a continuation of my comment from before. Or maybe it was a reminder that this wasn't a relationship.

Either way... "Thank every star in the sky. Keep your vote."

He took our masks and put them on a tall shelf before coming back to look me over. "This probably isn't a healthy way to go about our feud."

"We're feuding?"

"Are you going to talk the whole time?" Piper asked,

giving me another flashback to being alone in his room. "If I want healthy choices, I'll go to the ship's surgeon. Are you in, or not?"

"I'm in." I thought about the booze, something he rightfully called out. At this moment, I didn't care about anything beyond us being two consenting adults. "Desperately in. I just hope I come first this time so I can leave early."

Piper cracked up, and I grew warm all over. No one ever laughed at my jokes. They always claimed I was too dry in the delivery. Or, maybe—honestly, I didn't care as he pulled my hips flush with his, swaying us as one to the music I could barely still hear.

"You musical heathen," I said, pushing him back towards the clothes. "It's a coat check. Strip."

"Make me," he dared, leaning so far back into the racks I thought he might fall over. Instead, he simply faded from view as he brushed past and behind all the fabric.

I moved coats aside and realized just how large this closet was. I'd known it was a walk-in, but I never expected so many furs and coats to be held within here. The storage space even went further back along the side. There was a passing thought to the guild's storage needs as Piper traversed deeper, like he would find a rabbit hole in the back of it.

"Shit," he said and turned around. "Dead end."

I glanced over my shoulder before smiling back at him. There was plenty of room to stand here. And I thought we were fairly hidden unless someone really looked for us. "Now you have to listen to me."

Piper gestured down at his coat. "You call this following your instructions?"

I stepped close so I could start unbuttoning his

waistcoat. The jacket didn't clasp, so I could just push it off his shoulders later. Piper watched until his silence finally caused me to glance up. Our mouths were so close that neither of us could resist what was bound to happen next.

His mouth was hot, hungry, and relentless, only slowing as my lips parted with a gasp. His fingers sank into my hair in a refusal to let us part. My body prickled with anticipation, but there was still too much fabric between us. Left to blindly tug off whatever I felt, I didn't care if it ended up wrinkled in a pile on the floor.

Our pants required us to take a step back before we stood without a stitch in a closet full of finery. He stared at me, and I realized I hadn't been naked at all the last time.

"Not a word," I commanded.

Piper opened his mouth before deciding he would rather kiss me again. His hands roamed, stroking along my thigh. His fingers were a teasing whisper before taking both of our dicks into one hand, stroking up and down. I had never had a hand job pressed against another before, but now I was absolutely sure it was my new favorite thing. I moaned from the feeling, losing track of time, and grew frustrated as I heard footsteps outside.

"Cover my mouth," Piper said suddenly.

"What?"

Piper tilted his head down between us. "My hands are full, and I don't want to get yelled at for making noise. Cover my mouth if—"

I didn't need another second before shutting him up. It was an awkward two-handed grab after realizing he must have heard footsteps too. One palm was pressed to Piper's mouth while the second was at the base of his head so I could maintain pressure in the first place. It didn't do anything for me, but Piper's eyes went unfocused, breathing carefully through his nose as a muffled groan vibrated under my palm. The best and worst part was that his hands hadn't stopped moving. I became dizzy with pleasure and almost forgot to be quiet until the closet door opened.

Piper tensed. I heard the coat hangers shift and pressed our bodies further back into the far wall. His hands fell away so they didn't get trapped between us, and it all turned into an accidental grind.

Piper mumbled as I pinned us in place, but I didn't let up. I only slightly leaned to the side to spot where exactly the guest who walked in was through the fabrics. I could barely hear Piper over the sound of another person coming in.

"Ready to go?" a light voice called from the door.

"Yeah," the man shrugged on his jacket, and they both left us alone once more.

Only after I heard the door close did I drop my hands away and back off. "Sorry, what were you trying to say?"

Piper slouched, finally able to take a full breath again. "I said I'm going to come if you keep rubbing into me."

"Ah." I glanced over to him, privates still out on display, and blushed, knowing I wasn't any more appropriate for the public. Fear of actually being caught made me forget what we had been doing. "Sorry."

"Stop apologizing, and take me back to your place."

CHAPTER EIGHT
- PIPER -

I would've liked to say I jumped his bones the second we got somewhere private. But I became distracted by the manor he lived in. It was like a historic society showroom. "Is none of this yours?"

"No," Finch said, "I got rid of most of my things when I moved in."

"That's a dangerous game," I said.

From the outside, this place looked large, old, and stuffy. Appearances were misleading since the inside was full of stuff even more extreme, and there was enough of it that the place seemed small. They did not lay the space out for best use but rather angled it towards people passing by. There was not a speck of dust, but nothing was naturally piled up as if Finch lived here.

"How is free housing a risk?"

I turned to him, and he looked clueless about such things. *Selfless to a fault.* "I don't mean that part. More so, making your whole life dedicated to work. If you don't get re-elected, you'll have less than you started with."

He frowned, and I mirrored the expression instantly. This was his night to shine. We were having fun. This could still be fixed. I pushed him back with a passionate kiss, and he winced as we bumped into a table.

His gasp was a pleasing surprise that he turned into a nip at my lip as if to make us even. His hands roamed over my clothes, and I desperately wanted to feel his fingers on my skin.

"We're going to be black and blue by morning," I warned.

"Good. It will add to your existing color."

He pulled me deeper into the manor. It was dark without candles, and we continued to collide into various pieces of furniture as if it was all included on the tour.

"*Damn,*" Finch groaned against my mouth. His word was laced with another string of pain and coiled desire.

The combination made me not pay attention to our surroundings either. This front room was an obstacle course when moving blindly, and if we didn't fall at least onto a couch soon, I might just fuck him on the floor. It was all rather funny, and I fought back my amusement to keep my lips on his beautifully tanned skin. With our hands laced, he directed me upstairs to where I prayed was a bedroom.

We left a trail of clothes after we passed under a doorway. I tugged off his shirt before Finch hopped out of his shoes, and I couldn't stop myself from smirking. I wanted to tease more out using my tongue, not only for words, but to explore the hot skin I just uncovered. But his hand caught under my chin, lifted it, and stole my breath away. It was not tight enough to add pain, but I paused to remember to breathe.

"Do you find my eagerness funny?" he asked.

"About as much as you find mine." I pulled him closer to feel every line of his body, his erection pressed into my leg. "This better be your bedroom."

His coy smile verged delighted. "Maybe."

"Tease."

He pushed on my chest enough to imply what I should do next. By trust, I fell back and landed safely on a bed. Fairly comfortable one at that too, apart from the footboard against the top of my legs. It was such a relief to land somewhere soft.

I shimmed out of my pants. Finch removed his remaining clothes before he laid down next to me, and I turned on my side so we were face to face. Our detour here slowed us down, but our kisses now lingered too. They were tender and nowhere near the fanatic style from the closet.

I could fall asleep in the quiet safety of his room. Well, after *'dessert'*.

"Hey," he softly prompted, "what were we doing before?"

"What, frotting?"

"Frotting," he repeated as if it was a seating chart to memorize.

Finch's hand moved down towards our hips. But there was a tension in how rigid his fingers were. A struggle that seemed to need encouragement rather than a joke about Hamelin's questionable sex-ed classes.

"You don't have to still love me in the morning," I said, unable to avoid joking. "It's okay."

He smiled, even grinned as I sharply inhaled when he rubbed against my hard cock with the rocking of his hips. "Who says I love you now?"

Finch seemed to make it a personal challenge to fuck against me, as if wanting to get me off by the sheer friction of his erection. It was amazing as much as it was maddeningly teasing. And *oh,* was it *so* satisfying when he licked mindlessly along my collarbone. Our bodies fell into sync, catching that dance we missed.

My mouth moved to kiss and lick along the salty skin under his ear. My breaths timed a quick beat, and I was so delighted he decided to stick to this method where I was able to hold him close, leaning my forehead against his as we passed soft whines of pleasure between each other like they were secrets.

"You feel amazing," Finch all but moaned. "Sorry, I can't take another second."

Not sure why he was apologizing. Finishing was usually why you started. The moment after, I realized he meant our positions as he pushed me onto my back.

Finch placed a knee at each side of my hips as he came with a pump of his hand, and I shivered as heavy spurts hit my stomach. My hand slid over to grab myself and made a bigger mess along the way.

"I got you, Piper." His hand stroked me until my back arched off the bed. "If that's even your true name."

Who needed names at all? I started to seep into his hand, utter control of myself lost.

"*There* you go, handsome," he added and didn't let up. "Just like that."

I was whining, panting, and twitching so hard I thought my leg was about to cramp, and now I truly couldn't tell whose what was where on me. It was a sticky, delicious mess.

"Stars, look what I did to you."

Normally, I would have had more spunk to retort back. But we'd been edging closer to this moment for over an hour now, and my head needed to first remember where the blood went when it wasn't busy making me hard.

"What am I?" I asked, needing a breath. "Your cum rag?"

Finch let out a nervous laugh. "Sorry... I didn't want to wash the sheets after."

Even as I cussed at him, Finch still decided to golden rule the clean-up effort before he fell back on the bed.

"For the record," I smiled. "I don't hate myself. I hate *you*."

"That good, aye?" Finch teased, giving my words earlier tonight back to me.

We pulled back on our underwear, both silently deemed that enough for the night. I was more awake than ever, so I opted to lazily drag my fingers through his coppery brown hair. It looked better messed up. I wasn't sure if he was spent or just a heavy sleeper, but Finch was sound asleep while I thought back over what he said about my name.

"Oliver, by the way." My comment seemed only to have been heard by me, and that was alright. "It's been nice to meet you."

A voice called across a meadow. I wasn't sure what it said or where I was. But it was someplace bright and cheerful.

"Ollie, Ollie, oxen free!" This time, I recognized the words along with the voice. *It was Finch.*

I spun around, the sun comfortably warming my skin, feeling like a child playing a game. That was the last time I used my given name. It was still true in some ways, and not in others. Only people carrying magic seemed to know what I meant, so I never bothered to explain.

The field faded away as my eyes opened to see Finch gently shaking me awake. Groggy and half asleep, I still couldn't help but wonder. "What did you say?"

"Alle, alle auch sind frei," Finch repeated. "Means 'all, all, also are free.' It's just what we say when you want someone to stop messing around."

I curled into the blankets. "How am I goofing off while sleeping?" He didn't remember what I said, and hopefully, I could go back asleep and forget this conversation too.

"You're in my bed," Finch continued, losing his gentle tone. "Would you please get out of here?"

"Geez, fine." I sat up and found the rest of my clothes conveniently still on the floor. "Why can't I sleep in? Do you give tours to your bedroom?"

"Because I don't want you spotted when you leave for the day."

I pulled on my shirt and needed an extra second to make sure I didn't mess up the buttons. "Why are you so rude to me this morning?"

"Because I'm going to have a panic attack if we don't get going."

"What *we*?" I grumbled. I didn't think he heard over his anxiety, so I corrected myself. "What's the hurry?"

"There's maybe five minutes before this *public* building is open to the actual public during the day."

"Fuck'n *start* with that next time!"

CHAPTER NINE
- FINCH -

I didn't know where Piper went after we barely made it out of the manor without suspicion. I didn't see anyone nearby, and it wasn't like that was a hot spot. Still, small towns were quite gossipy.

There had been a grumbled goodbye after he had reminded me I was meant to get Ms. Whitefall coffee, and I hated the idea because it would–*and did*–end up making me late to the office.

Lana was sitting in the chair in front of my desk when I finally made it there. I offered her the second cup as a peace offering for making her wait.

"Morning. Please, sit?" Lana said, rising to grab the mug before we both took our respective spots. "About last night..."

Did she mean the open flirting with Piper? Leaving the party early? Or the completely sober hook-up that I was just now getting back from? I shuffled the papers around on my desk and pretended a flier for a kid's camping trip needed my focus. "What about it?"

"You did wonderfully! Everyone had a great time and felt like you were social with them. I should apologize," she said.

I met her eyes and broke into a cold sweat. She had

never said sorry—never *needed* to do such a thing.

"I kept pushing you and pushing you to engage more with people. You managed to loosen up on your own, and everyone seemed to like that."

Shock kept me from replying. *Was this a dream?*

"Anyway," she said as she stood up. "Good job, and thank you for the coffee."

"You're welcome."

I didn't see Piper for a whole two days after that. I asked at the inn, but he wasn't there. I just learned that he paid ahead until the end of the week. Then, I headed towards the docks to see if there were any ships before finally going back to my office so I wasn't late for another meeting.

On the way back, I caught the sight of the moon hanging in the sky. It was still there, so he really should've been somewhere here as well.

Halfway into my meeting with two members of the merchant's guild, Piper walked into my office like he owned the place. I glanced over like he was just going to hand me something, but he sat down on the corner of the desk. Once the man in front of us stopped speaking, Piper leaned into my space.

"You think you are so fucking cute," he hissed, "Have you ever—"

"Please give us a moment!" *Nope!* Nope, nope. This was not a safe-for-work conversation.

I grabbed him by the wrist, yanked him out of my office, and pushed him into a supply closet. It was tiny and cramped, but I didn't trust him enough not to blurt something out in the hallway. The door was not even secured behind us, but I couldn't figure out Piper's hard-set glare. "What's the matter?"

"Ask before you touch me again, asshole," Piper complained as he fixed his clothes.

"What are you doing here?"

"You see, I thought 'our business' was done," Piper said. "But then I asked the good people of Hamelin and learned that your little town has outlawed sex work, making what we first did together not a payment. I see as you truly are now: pretending you're moral, while doing what your people don't have the freedom to mirror."

"You can't f—" I cut myself off, knowing I shouldn't cuss in this building. "I thought you traveled with pirates. Surely you know a deal's a deal."

"The law is the law, *Mayor.*" Piper's green eyes glimmered with a dark amusement I hadn't seen before. "So what will it be? Confess your crimes, or live with the fact that you sucked me off for the pure pleasure of it and *still* owe me a ton of money?"

I stared at the space between us, trying to figure out how to get myself out of this situation. I was also reeling over how I was suddenly *in* it. "You hate hypocrites."

"Yeah." Piper pushed past me towards the door. "Maybe I should ask those fine folks for their opinion on it?"

"I'm up for re-election, and they are the leaders of the merchant guilds. I'd be screwed either way."

"Then tell me the truth, or am I just some scum brought in by pirates?" Piper sneered, fighting to keep his volume low enough for even the chance of this remaining a secret.

My hand scrubbed down my face. "Fine, it did start as a stupid idea to get you to leave town quickly. I may have allowed it to get out of hand."

Piper snickered like I told a dirty joke.

"Will you please go for now? We can talk later."

"Sure thing." He bumped into my shoulder on his way out. I followed into the hallway and watched as he stopped near the door.

"But you still gotta pay me!" Piper yelled. Now *that* was surely loud enough for everyone to overhear. *Damn it.*

"Mayor Finch!" a voice called from the front door. Whoever it was ignored Ms. Whitefall's objections to wait in the lobby. When I stepped out, Angela nearly collided with me, her hands grabbing both my shoulders as if terrified I wouldn't listen.

"I never see you here. What's wrong?"

She didn't look bruised or harmed, aside from her frantic demeanor. I eyed the door to see if her husband was following.

"You gotta listen to me," she said as her hands gripped tighter. "The kids are missing!"

"Maybe they are at a friend's house?"

"No! All the kids," she said. "Every last one in town is gone!"

"Show me?"

Quicker than I could have snapped my fingers, she headed out the door. In the square outside Town Hall, several parents called out their kids' names or discussed amongst themselves. The overlap of voices repeated a few details, but they seemed uncertain of plenty. The only consistent detail was that everyone's kids were up and out of the house before dawn.

"Do you think it's the piper?" Angela asked me. Her tone hadn't been very loud, but the idea burned through the crowd in a flash.

"Yeah! That mage did this!" yelled a voice.

"Was our money not good enough?" another said. "How much will the ransom for the children be?"

"Everyone! Everyone!" I moved up the stairs that overlooked the square, trying to use the extra height to get their attention. "Whatever is going on, we will figure it out. I assure you."

A new hand touched my arm, and I turned around, full of hope it was Piper. Then this would be cleared up. Instead, Lana was standing there with a concerned expression.

"Go," she said. "I'll organize a search."

I did my best to avoid any parents or people who might've had questions until I had the answers. The tavern had another group of parents, and with the rumor mill running, I doubted Piper would stay amongst them. He also was conspicuously missing from his room at the inn. Given his attitude earlier, I very much started to think he might have been responsible for this. A thousand guilders from me was an impossible task, but a few from each parent could be raised by evening.

Along the waterfront was the only place I hadn't checked. Despite feeling like I had already checked it once today, I ventured back. A lone silhouette waiting out on the pier casually skipping rocks gave Piper away. I marched up and grabbed a fistful of his shirt without so much as a hello.

"Your pranks have gone too far this time!"

Piper's balance wavered, but not before he laughed at my weak threat of pushing him into the water. "Missing something, Mayor?"

"How *could* you?" My eyes stung after putting so much trust in a stranger that had only shown up to collect a large sum of money. *Were these his true colors?*

"How could I *what?*" Piper sneered as he ripped my hand away. "What am I now to your fearful city?"

The words on my tongue felt like molasses I had to push through. "Looking like the villain."

"Let's see you win the parental vote when everyone is busy searching for their kids." His grin grew wicked. "Is that demographic worth double since people often share the same children?"

"Tell me where the kids are!"

"Make me," he dared. This time, the words weren't suggestive, nor even mean. *They sounded hurt.*

I stepped back and wondered if I knew the man in front of me at all.

"What compelled you to even think I could summon children anywhere? They are their own people, you know."

"Of course, I know that!" My volume didn't dip, but my resolve slipped. If Piper hadn't been the one to take every child out of town, who had they followed? I needed him to be honest with me. Now, more than ever.

"What is this to you, Finch?" Piper asked. Within the question was a subject change that I couldn't afford right now.

"If it wasn't you…" The comment was more to myself

than him as I studied his face. Piper always looked out of place here. Now, he was just a man at a dead end waiting for someone across the water to draw close enough to shore so he could leave. "If the papers knew everything, they'd call you a distracting gold digger."

"The papers? Are you an imbecile that doesn't realize that wasn't my question?" Piper chastised. "Stop looking at me like some lost puppy and answer my question."

"I don't know!" I took a breath as my heart beat unevenly. "How could I even think about anything else when all the children are missing?"

He rolled his eyes. "Are you a father?"

"What? No."

Piper stepped around me to brush past again. I turned to grab his hand and barely remembered he told me not to touch him. I had just enough time to pull up short. Piper lifted his arm away, assuring that I'd miss either way. But there was a silent moment where we both realized this; catching myself somehow earned me his pity.

"Then why is their care your responsibility?"

I still didn't understand what he meant. But I knew it was a clue somehow. The genuine answer was just under the surface, if only I could see clearly enough. But Piper didn't stick around to help me figure it out and headed back into town.

"Why do mages need riddles?" I shouted out over the waves.

I didn't even realize Piper had stopped at the end of the pier until I turned and saw him there. His arms were out wide as if to say *'come on'* with a breathless stare.

"You're the most unintelligent, smart person I've ever known," he yelled back. "You can help find the kids, but after that consider it war between us."

Piper walked off. Even after I called his name, he just waved me off and kept going. With no other choice besides asking the ocean again, my path took me back until I slumped down into my office chair.

And then I saw the answer. *The camping flier.* It had been near the top of the papers because it included a change that needed approval. One that hadn't been pointed out, and I hadn't spotted on my own. *The date was for today.* The trip had been moved up, and everyone just feared the worst after so much hardship before and uncertainty now.

"Ms. Whitefall!" I called out. Maybe I also needed adult supervision not to fuck up my life. It took her a moment before she stepped into my office and took the flier from my extended hand. "Spread the news that the camp chaperone took the kids out early."

She didn't seem to believe me at first. Not that I'd trust an idiot like me, either. If I'd been paying better attention…

"This shouldn't have gone through," she said. Her eyes finally lifted off the paper and to me. "He's not allowed to make changes like this so fast. You're… more observant than I gave you credit for, Mayor Finch."

I barely managed a smile. "Please start letting the parents know."

It seemed I didn't ruin my political career, just the one relationship I wanted for myself.

CHAPTER TEN
- PIPER -

Sure, *blame the mage.* Everyone always blamed the mage. If something couldn't be explained—even if something could—fearful people found it easier to blame magic. Admitting that people were different from them was somehow too hard of a truth. We were too difficult to control.

Maybe that was why mages got blamed. We were vagabonds untied to anything and freer than they ever wanted to be. But it was particularly ignorant to blame a summoner. The only logic it held was surface deep. People were the hardest to summon. Let alone a hundred and thirty at once.

What I could do, however, was annoy them all. My first victim was the camp counselor that had moved up a camping trip in hopes of more favorable weather. He was more of a bystander, punished to stay within the town square for two days, already doing the penance of—well, I didn't honestly care. Looked like recycling.

"If you play that same earworm for a third day," he seemed to warn as I returned to my spot dead in the center of the square.

"You'll do what?" I dared.

My goal was to annoy Mayor Finch, who now had

people coming in and out of Town Hall all day long. All the building's windows were facing the square, so I knew everyone inside could hear. It was an infectious little tune. I heard people hum it to themselves as I passed, only to bemoan that it was stuck in their head's moments later. The fact that the real culprit was also stuck listening should have been a bonus for Hamelin.

I played the same song over and over as if it never had an end. Even when I did stop for the day, the birds started singing it to each other. On the evening of the third day, Mayor Finch came out. He nodded a strained acknowledgment to the man stuck doing community service for scaring everyone.

"How are you today, Piper?" Finch asked.

"That depends."

He attempted to hold back a sigh. "On what?"

"How are you doing?"

A frown crossed his face. "Piper..."

"Yes, Mayor Finch?"

He glanced up at the sky, looking for help from stars that weren't out yet. Then, compelled by some duty, he held out a proclamation of sort out towards me. "I thought it would be best if you heard it from me."

I grabbed the paper out of his hands and studied the flowing ink that had his signature along the bottom. My surprise made it a struggle to read, as if I had grown illiterate.

"Music without a permit can no longer be played in public," Finch summarized.

The stranger sorting tin at my side collapsed next to his pile in relief.

"Oh, go cry wolf!" I shot him a dirty look before glaring at the Mayor. "You're not the one being picked on."

Finch carefully took the document from me. Which was fine because what in all the lands was I meant to do with a law like this? "No one is trying to pick on you, Piper."

"You didn't simply outlaw music. You *targeted* me!"

His somber expression tensed over my volume. "You never gave me a name apart from your job, and it's not only about you, so I had to be careful with my wording. You not being guilty doesn't change the fact that everyone is now aware of the influence magic and music can do together."

My voice held a growl before it even sounded like words. "It only applies to me."

"Only because you're the only musical mage in town."

I glared at Finch. "Did you even consider apologizing?"

"Of course, but you've still been driving everyone mad."

"Deeply true," the camp counselor mumbled. Metal clanged against the rest of the pile after he finished cleaning it out of whatever food was leftover. "Practically lost my marbles in this pile."

"Shut up!" We both said in unison, and the counselor piped down fast, eyes widening in surprise over his lack of allies. I resented that the Mayor and I had just agreed.

My silent stare down resumed since, apparently, playing music in public was now illegal. I'd always been able to see a glimmer of something joyful in Finch's eyes. A playful flame that was easy to feed, but now he was just pathetically laughable.

"You're *so* mad at me." Finch winced, looking mortally wounded by my sole opinion.

It was nauseating. He didn't care about me. Definitely not over any other soul in town. "Of course I'm mad at you! You called me a gold digger and then outlawed my one talent."

"Technically, I said that's what others would say. And this?" Finch gestured to the paper in his hand. "It was for public safety. Plus, it's not like it's your *only* talent."

How dare he try to revive our flirtatious game as if he hadn't killed it.

"Piper, come on. I'm sure you'll find some clever way to outwit me tomorrow."

I thought—What did it matter what I thought if Finch didn't realize that music and magic were so deeply personal to me?

"No, fuck off. Find someone else to harass."

Neither of them said anything else as I left the square. The pirates should be back tonight. If Warren wasn't in a rowboat soon ready to pick me up, I would swim across the sea just to leave this place.

Knowing what it feels like to wait, Warren was on time. He was a good enough man that he didn't even comment on me making quick work to row back to the ship. As we rejoined the pirates on the main deck, I noticed the dried paint drops on Warren's clothes.

"Do you think I could commission you to paint something for me?" I asked.

The rest of my coins were here. Maybe everything could be solved by throwing money at my problems. If I couldn't use music to showcase my feelings, visual arts were certainly a worthy replacement.

"Sure?" Warren said and convinced me to explain what

I was looking for in his cabin. Never being a social butterfly among the pirates, I was happy with a one-on-one audience where I could explain why I came back empty-handed.

To describe my idea, I had to end up telling Warren why I was annoyed at Finch. The only problem was that Warren shared his cabin with the Captain, who stepped in and only caught the tail end of the conversation.

"Why don't you return once this one is finished?" Captain Hook said. His hand raised towards a canvas that Warren had been working on. The painting showed trees and a mountainous landscape that looked unfinished as he focused on the enormous castle.

"But Cap'n, I want something that gracefully showcases me being metaphorically sucked off by my now diametrically opposed political opponent."

Hook's laugh is undoubtedly dangerous, sexy, and with dark humor. If the reviews were true, he'd make for a night no one could ever forget. Doubted I could use it to make Finch jealous, however.

Warren accessed his work before turning back to us, brush still in hand. "You both know that this is a castle, right?"

"You know what? Perfect! The mayor doesn't have a castle. Do not stop painting for the world." I sat down on the edge of the bed, determined to wait here until Warren was finished.

Hook's lip curled. "That isn't where you belong."

"Spoilsport," I verbally bit back, even as I got off the mattress.

Captain Hook grunted, and I didn't even try to assume what it meant before he picked Warren up as easily as a sack of cargo.

Warren wrapped around Hook's hips as if born to be there. "Goodness, I missed you too," Warren said before he smiled brightly.

Hook didn't reply before kissing the man rough enough that I feared for the air in my own lungs.

"Alright, I'm going, I'm going!" I said as I stepped out before it got any more heated.

Instantly, I ran into Smee on the other side of the door and nearly jumped out of my skin.

"What do you want with them?" she asked, clearly protective of her unkillable captain and his well-loved mage.

It was so laughable that it was practically a joke, so I just winked at her.

"I outta hang you up by your breeches," Smee threatened. "Then you'll give me a straight answer."

"I don't do anything straight, lass."

She moved to the side when I tried to slip past her, and she stayed directly in front of me no matter which direction I went. It was a bothersome little dance, so I just caved.

"This is annoying," I sighed. "Keep your mind out of the gutter. I was updating them about business. Now, let me get back to it if you ever want to see a single guilder from me."

"You've changed," Smee decreed.

"Uh-huh," I replied and tested if she'd let me pass.

She did but not without speaking again. "The old Piper would have claimed he could go all night."

I couldn't believe I was on this stupid ship with a bunch of freaking pirates I couldn't seem to break free from. "Maybe I'm tired of the dance's steps."

"Maybe you found a dedicated dance partner."

Smee's own bunk-related fun times were a mystery to me, so I knew she wasn't talking about our dynamic. But I loathed how Finch's smell clung to me. "How fast would you save me if I threw myself overboard?"

"For a bath?" she asked and rubbed a hand along her chin. "Not until you're soaked through."

"Good to know."

She threw an arm over my shoulder and directed me with her weight around to where she wanted me to go. "You should get some shut eye first. Doesn't that work for mages who've gone mad?"

My steps stalled out a step below deck. "You mean the thing people call sleeping?"

Smee grinned, and I caught the gap between her front teeth. It was a smile rarer than a blue moon. *She was fucking with me.* I laughed for a second and felt better as the tension in my chest broke apart.

CHAPTER ELEVEN
- FINCH -

The tavern went quiet as I stepped in. All discussions halted, and the clinking cheers of mugs subsided as every eye turned toward me. I definitely wouldn't have wanted to poll this group to find out my popularity. Piper's eyes were among the watchful crowd. At least until they rolled away, as he turned his back to me when I started walking in his direction. I wasn't sure if he'd been bad-mouthing me, or telling the truth, or if a silence held more than both. I hadn't been right to let Piper even indirectly take any of the blame. That degree had merit, but annoying someone wasn't a crime.

"Drinking to forget?" I asked, with a nod toward his drink.

"It's coffee, you selected narc." Piper's eyes stayed on the back wall and refused to find mine.

"Can I sit?"

"Free city," Piper said, taking a long sip before putting the mug down. "Well, free-ish city."

"Are you planning on being civil?" I asked softly. He came back to town. That alone felt like a miracle I didn't deserve, and I wasn't going to waste it.

"Sure."

I pressed my lips together, knowing he was being unusually careful with his words around me. "Do you want to be? Can't say I'd blame you after everything."

Piper suddenly turned in his seat. I was hopeful that he'd say something, *anything*, that would give me a look into why he was back or how he was feeling. But there was nothing but an incredulous stare.

"Let me make this right," I begged. "1,000 guilders isn't impossible right now. What can I give you? What do you *need?*"

Piper glanced back at his drink, running a finger around the rim of the mug. "Ten percent."

"100 guilders?" My voice lifted with surprise. I could probably do that.

Piper nodded as he continued to look ahead. "Promised the pirates that much for the ride."

Did he owe the pirates, or did his code of ethics just demand he gave what he promised even if he was shorted in the process? That didn't matter. I didn't need to know to do what I should have done already.

"Okay. I'll figure it out. Come by my office this afternoon."

Piper looked over his shoulder as he brooded. If he could summon a storm, I think there'd be a rain cloud over his head.

"No funny business. I'll have the ten percent," I said, praying he'd find some faith in me again. "If you decide that's not enough, then consider it just a down payment."

The bartender stepped over, eyeing me cautiously. "Can I get you something, Mayor?"

"No, thank you." I smiled up at her, but she didn't return one. "I'll see you later, Piper?"

"Yeah, noon or whatever."

Minutes ago, Lana brought all the coins she had at home to add to the existing money I had gathered already. Of course, that had been paired with a speech about how I should have just been honest with her in the first place.

'Noon or whatever' turned out to be almost exactly noon. Like Piper had been outside beforehand and the sun was the last push that finally made him show up. Not that I was watching, or bemoaning his arrival, since I had needed the entire morning. I had to mind my smile as he appeared in the doorway. He seemed in a better mood, but his default smile faded upon seeing me.

"Would you like a seat?"

He sat down, slouching a bit with his legs spread out.

"I am sorry that I thought the misunderstanding was your doing," I started, but that didn't seem to get a single reaction out of him. "Also, that I didn't say this sooner. And that even calling everything a misunderstanding sounds oddly dismissive. I miss your music, and your smile, and I'm so sorry."

His eyes widened before a chuckle escaped. "Okay."

The silence between us grew uncomfortably long until I remembered he came to finally be paid. *Right...*

I cleared my throat. "The money is in the cabinet next to you."

He glanced over, and I realized I still had to get up and unlock it. There was a passing idea to just give him the key before I hastily got up to take care of it all myself. As I bent down to unlock it, my anxiety over everything turning awkward only increased. I thought he was silently staring at me.

There was a nervous sheen over my face as I stood back up and offered the coin purse. Piper's eyes lifted to mine briefly before taking the money. When he sat back down, relief flooded me.

"Is it weird I almost thought you'd smack my ass there?"

"Are you cussing in the office now?" Piper raised a brow before adding another question. "Was I supposed to?"

"No. It's just…" *Didn't matter.* I shook my head and sat back down.

"Tell me," Piper insisted as he opened the coin purse and counted the coins on the desk. "Please."

The prospect felt as daunting as finding 100 guilders in a single morning. But he seemed willing to hold a conversation now, at least. "You're so forward sometimes. I guess I just expected it."

Piper didn't even look up as he spoke. "I'm surprisingly not into ass."

"Really?"

Piper nodded without a worry about what anyone thought about that fact. It was likely something we should have discussed *before* fooling around together, not *after* committing to being enemies.

"You know what?" I leaned forward like we shared a secret. "Me neither."

"Yeah?" Piper added, busy making groups of ten as he counted.

I nodded and watched him. "Always feels like it needs so much more effort to get ready for it. I don't feel like I have the time for it all when there's…" Our time together flashed in my mind, replaying like the moment before the death of our could-have-been relationship, which left me further flushed. "Other things."

"That's a very *you* answer." Piper laughed and lost count at an eight and had to recount a stack. His comment sounded like it *should* have been cruel but wasn't somehow. There was a casual acceptance of whatever. It was just Piper being Piper, really.

"Alright. Well, what's your reason?"

"Don't need one; I just don't," Piper shrugged, then gestured to the dozen piles and change left over. "There's more than you said here."

"It's 12.2%. It's mostly from a livery collar I'm meant to display. The front case will look a little bare for a while, but it was a gift for *me* so…" As I trialed off, Piper glanced down as if wanting to recount again. "I didn't want you to end up with less than you started with."

Piper grew pale. "Don't do that."

"Don't do what?"

"Don't try to be the person I thought you were."

CHAPTER TWELVE
- PIPER -

How *dare he try to get me to like him after everything?* Before I lost my head, I slid the coins off the desk and back into the small leather purse. If I returned to the harbor fast, I could catch the pirates before they set sail again.

"You were right," Finch said.

He was still standing in the way to leave the office, and probably didn't even notice. I could have pushed past, but I was afraid to get closer. I had liked him before, and I didn't know if I could trust myself not to pick up the habit once more.

"Screw you; pay me the rest."

"Pick one," he said roughly, a perfect match for my tone.

That was a weird thing to say, and it threw me off enough that, even as he moved back to his desk, I just stood around watching him as he tossed official-looking papers across his desk.

"I made sex work legal. You were right," he repeated. "I was being a hypocrite, and I also despise people like that in politics. This is all I could do to not hate myself. Sometimes there are trade-offs in politics, but I no longer care about those who decry the act."

"What the fuck?" There was a tight feeling in my stomach, and I told myself it was the coffee's fault. *Was it possible to have a panic attack over good news?* "I was just messing around. I didn't mean to… bring about anything."

"I know, but it was the right thing to do."

"Will you lift the public music ban?"

"No, give it a beat." He took a breath, still struggling under the weight of what everyone wanted. "I'm sure people will realize the truth and celebrate you with your very own day soon enough."

I shifted my weight between my two feet, unable to find a comfortable position. "Will you let me have a pet rat in town?"

"Okay."

I blinked at the Mayor, trying to see the logic in the enforcement. "Really?"

"Bell can be grandfathered in," Finch said. And I couldn't find a way to argue because he did seem to have the authority to declare such things. "Does this mean you'll be staying in town?"

I smoothed the jacket over my chest, suddenly warm. "I'm going to need you to stop looking at me like that."

"Like what?"

"Like you know I hate you, yet you still can't wait until I let you touch me again."

Finch's mouth parted to lick his lips. It was a nervous habit, but it still made me hope for what he'd say next as he became tongue-tied. "Please stay until the election. Give us a chance to start right."

Hamelin wasn't a terrible place to be while waiting for your ship to come in. Drama faded fast, and people talked their fears out. Election day landed on the new moon, and I wasn't sure if our stars were crossed yet. But, after spending a month at the inn, I was leaving with more than I came here with.

Just as I pushed my trunk closed, I heard footsteps at my door. "You're still here," Finch panted, looking out of breath after running in from town.

"Still here," I answered back.

Today was when we got to know the results of his re-election. We'd planned to spend more time together over the past month, but we only managed to re-build enough trust that I could admit that I'd vote for him—if I could. Didn't want election fraud drama in my life. I probably could have demanded time together, made him pick me over the time spent on his campaign, but I thought he was the best man for the job. *So…*

"Are you owed congratulations, Mayor?"

"I, um." He swallowed roughly as I ventured closer. The other thing we worked back up to was touching. Not *that* type yet, but the sort where we'd find ourselves shoulder to shoulder whenever we sat side-by-side. Both of us seemed to breathe easier if we shared the other's space.

Since I had closed the distance, he was the one who picked up my hands. Thumbs ran across my knuckles as he worked up the courage to finish speaking. I held my heart back from leaping out of my chest.

"I haven't checked," Finch continued. "When I woke

up, all I could think of was you. If I lost, I wouldn't have less than before because I met you. Losing *you* would be worse than missing out on my job. I do want to win; I want to win badly. But I want it to be with you at my side."

My stomach stirred with butterflies, and if I opened my mouth, they might fly out.

"Piper, I love you."

"Is that what our fairytale is meant to be?" I squeezed his hands, trying to picture it. "The rat catcher of Hamelin moves into the Mayor's manor?"

"Could be." His voice sounded like a wish as he drew me closer into a hug.

My head rested on his shoulder, eyes still on the window-framed horizon. "I'd walk around that precious historical building in nothing but my birthday suit."

"I hope you do," he whispered and didn't let go.

"What if a dog wins?"

"Don't think pets mind nudity, but they couldn't appreciate it like me."

I smiled and pulled back to see his face to offer a remaining confession. "Stars, I love you too."

His eyes gleamed at my words, his grin growing wild and free.

There he was... "I haven't seen you smile like this since we first met."

"I was smiling when we first met?" he asked.

"You don't remember?"

Finch shook his head. "Found myself distracted at the time. I thought you were the most handsome man I ever saw. Then, you opened your mouth and were insufferably full of life. I've been smitten despite myself ever since."

"Stop flattering me, you scoundrel."

"*Make me.*"

I caught myself leaning into him again before I stopped fighting myself. Our breaths mixed before I pressed my lips to his, and he melted into my kiss. The torment of waiting stirred me to grab his hips and pulled him back until we reached the inn's bed. It was still mine for another hour or so.

And I was not content to even stop kissing until he was straddling my lap as I stared up at him.

"If we marry someday, *then* do I get to vote?"

"You think I'm going to let a criminal like you vote?" Finch teased as he nipped at my ear.

"What crime are you accusing me of this time?" I managed as my eyes fluttered closed as his mouth moved down my neck.

"Stealing my heart?"

"Not a crime." I grinned, knowing his words sounded like a question because it was *so* cheesy, and Finch absolutely knew that too.

"Sure it is." He sat up and gave me what was meant to be a very serious look that only made me smirk further. "I'm going to make it one."

"No, you're not." I sat up, trying to catch his mouth again, but his hand playfully held me back until I relented. "Have mercy? I couldn't help myself."

I shivered as his hand slipped under my clothes. His mouth dragged back up to mine, but I was the one who won a moan as I rocked my hips up into him. Finch cupped the sides of my face to further anchor him to me, and I realized that there was no way I was catching that ship today.

Every nerve tingled with a pleased excitement. Even as I flipped us around and moved down until Finch was the one writhing on the bed. His hips gently bucked to dive himself further into my mouth. Selfishly, I decided the prohibitions could stay as long as I was able to get drunk off the sounds this man made and how his ecstasy tasted spilled on the back of my tongue.

CHAPTER THIRTEEN
- FINCH -

According to Lana, Piper and I had a bit of a PDA problem. It didn't rise to the level of a scandal, however— also, according to her. Since the campaign was over, she returned to her non-election season job of managing school events. That was something that clearly needed her oversight more than we did.

Well, I suppose that depended on who you asked. Piper still couldn't summon within city limits, but he had a pet magically tethered to him as if on a long leash. That meant he worked on training the rat the old-fashioned way with tongue clicks and treat-sized bribes.

The creature ran across the floor and crawled up towards a purse hanging off the back of the chair. Its owner was busy talking to another woman in front of her and didn't notice as the rat jumped up. The little rodent climbed up enough to dig his nose in and pull out a banknote. When the rat dropped back to the ground, I swore the woman would see. As their conversation continued without a hitch, Bell ran back to our table.

"Piper," I said, shaking my head. "Knock it off."

"It seems you caught me. What are you going to do with me?" He smirked, knowing all our games ended with fun and sex.

"I'm going to return this." I carefully reached down to take the money from Bell before the creature ran to Piper's hand, still looking for his reward.

I walked over to the woman it had been taken from and commented she must have dropped the money. She appeared confused but thankful as she checked her purse. Maybe I should have made Piper cleanout recyclables in the public square. I never did, but that didn't mean he got off innocent either.

"Now what?" Piper asked, eager to find out.

"Hamelin doesn't send people to jail, so guess I'll have to punish you myself." My hand rested under my chin to think about it. "I can be lenient. What do you think is fair?"

His green eyes filled with mischief as I sat down. "I'd say a ticket," Piper answered, "but you already got *fine* written all over."

As I smile, he leaned in to capture my mouth with a quick kiss. "I still need to check my schedule."

"Don't you have breaks?" There was plenty of room for both of us, but he slid closer. The two of us were seemingly unable to avoid touching as our legs chastely aligned from hip to knee.

"I never remember to take them."

Piper leaned in again; head low as he spoke. "As long as you never forget to take me."

"You have a way with words." I was suddenly too warm under my collared shirt. I didn't know which season I fear more: winter for the added layers, or summer when they lack.

Late that afternoon, a new guest to Hamelin looked around in awe at all the bright colors of Hamelin's floral shop. All the flowers decorating the displays were in full bloom. Everything was naturally perfect for today's showcase. The florist himself was in the back carefully keeping himself busy at a comfortable distance.

"Welcome to town, Ms. Nabb. This is my side piece, Mayor Finch," Piper said, finishing his otherwise proper introduction to the farming representative.

She had a small frame with a few muscles. She likely preferred the travel and admin work that organizing needed over the daily duties of a farmhand. As first impressions went, her idea of sending extra perishables to a farmer's market sounded very appealing. Our florist was an anxious man with a green thumb that resulted in far more beauty than Hamelin needed for itself.

But first... I looked over at Piper. "That's not what I am."

"Sure it is. You recently won re-election," Piper said, beaming at the near stranger. "Isn't that exciting?"

She smiled back politely, and I stepped in before Piper started to brag about me. "Please ignore my boyfriend, who thinks he's very funny."

"Oh, you are together? You two should come out and try some of our avocados. The orchard is a great little place for a romantic getaway."

"We'd love to," Piper said. "You know, I always thought they tasted like clean—"

"Dear," I interrupted, hands quickly on his shoulders and ready to push him somewhere else. "I see Lana and

her daughter outside. Why don't you go say hello for us?"

The only thing Piper loved more than me was his attempts to embarrass me. My reaction was what he enjoyed because as soon as I wasn't there to hear a conversation, the crass jokes stopped.

"Sure thing," Piper said and kissed my cheek before he thankfully left me alone to talk to the nice farmer who did not need to know where that mouth had been.

Either blissfully innocent or extremely kind, Ms. Nabb said nothing about his comments. "What does your boyfriend do?"

"He's a musician."

"That's lovely," she said with a smile. "Maybe he can play at one of our farmer's markets?"

"I think he'd like that."

Her son ran up to her. He was a young boy with straw hair and already had more muscle than she did and attempted to nudge her along towards a miniature orchid near the register.

Ms. Nabb had a steady hand and hugged him to her side. "You thinking about having kids someday?"

I smiled at the two of them. "Maybe… if I get Piper to stop acting like one first."

She chuckled before extending her hand to shake my hand. "It was a pleasure meeting you, Mayor Finch. We'll talk more after I visit with Hamelin's other shop owners. If you'll excuse me, I think we need to go buy a plant."

"That all sounds great."

I was mildly stunned at how smooth that went. Piper *was* great for my ability to connect with other people. I now existed beyond my job and came off as more than just a cog within local government. Even the florist ventured out to tentatively mention the flower's water needs. I greeted Lana and her daughter as they stepped into the shop, and she mentioned Piper was still outside getting some air.

I found him leaning against a stone banister, gaze adrift out towards the sea. A lot of planning had gone into that meeting which only took a few minutes. It left me to wonder if my daily life was too boring for someone like him.

"Are you enjoying your day?"

"It's great. Just needed a moment to think."

"About what?" I asked and laced our fingers together.

"If I'm going to stay here, I need to get the rest of my stuff from the pirates."

There was a terrifying idea. Ms. Nabb had spent a week isolated with her son at the inn to put everyone's concerns about another plague to rest. Now more people would be coming from who knows where?

Piper squeezed my hand. "Do you trust me?"

"Yes, it's just—yes."

"Hamelin is my home now too. I won't do anything to harm it."

"I know. I'm just anxious."

"Come relax with me."

"How?" Kissing and chaste touches were fine, but I wasn't going to risk being caught doing more with families around.

"Let's go to bed early. We can meet them when they arrive early in the morning."

I end up pacing around the manor. It was a space that didn't fully feel like mine, and I was too wired with every possibility that could happen after today's events. Let alone everything else a pirate ship could bring to shore.

Piper watched me as he sat on an antique roll-top desk. There was no need to scold him to move since his pants didn't have any rivets to scratch the wood. "Come on, we agreed to bed."

He pushed off to stand, took my hand, and then brought me upstairs to what was now *our* room. Instead of demanding I change and continue the charade of getting ready for the night, his hand lifted mine as if I was meant to take a step on to the bed.

"Up," Piper directed. "We need to tire you out first."

My muscles tighten to finally find resistance to his suggestion. Even though I wasn't sure what he was suggesting. "Shouldn't we be *in* the bed?"

"No." Piper dropped my hand so he could have both arms for balance as he climbed on top. "We can still test if we can break the frame, if you'd like." He pushed up with the balls of his feet, and I realized belatedly that the suggestion was that we *jump* on the bed. Or maybe even dance around.

I carefully stepped up next to him, using his arm to help me first find my balance. "Think I'll need some music to be fully convinced to jump."

"I have your permission?"

My eyes dropped to his hip where the pipe always

stayed, just waiting to be played. "Don't need it for a song in private."

He pulled the instrument to his lips and blew the same tune I heard him humming in my office before. We bounced, danced, and outright jumped around on the bed, making a concert on the private island that was this mattress. I went harder since I didn't have to keep the music going. And a few songs later, I burned off my anxiety enough that I was actually pretty tired.

Shortly after the sun rose, we went to the coast. Someone on board must have been watching for us with a spyglass because after we arrived, a small rowboat was lowered into the water. Piper's pirate friend drew closer and pulled onto the land. He was a rather sober-looking man in every sense of that word. I didn't smell any rum as he neared, and the mage even seemed quite mindful to tilt his hat to keep the sun off his face.

He hadn't come with anyone else, but a large chest filled the other side of his small rowboat. It took the three of us to pull it out and onto the shore.

Once the heavy lifting was done, the pirate-mage finally took a moment to look me over. Afraid I'd make a terrible impression; I offered my hand out. "You must be the healer. Warren?"

The man glanced down at my hand, then at Piper, before finally shaking it. "Mayor Finch, I presume?"

"Yes." His tone was a careful neutral I also didn't expect for someone who spent his life as a pirate. "Excuse me, did I miss something?"

"Thought you were a germaphobe," Warren said. "Yet, you shook my hand."

"The plague we had wasn't largely spread with handshakes. Though, we do wash our hands often, just in case."

"Hmm," Warren said, sounding genuinely curious. "Good to know."

He turned and lightly kicked the side of the chest that looked comically pirate-like, as if a child drew it. But Piper could just as easily have kept spare underwear in it. "That's all of it."

Piper crouched down in front of the chest. "How is everyone going to fare without me?"

"Don't worry about us," Warren said. "The ocean treats us fairly."

When Piper lifted the lid, I felt as if a fever dream had set in. All the shining gold coins and gems almost made me go blind. "*Wow,* you have money! Like, a lot of money."

"That's because I never not got paid. Until *you.*" Piper reeled me in close as my shock lingered, and I couldn't even manage to take my eyes off of it. "Now who is the gold digger?"

It hardly mattered what he teased when he used that sexy tone and made me bemoan the existence of clothes and company.

"You run a food program here?" Warren asked me.

Piper pulled back, holding onto my hand, and gave me a nudge to answer.

"Yes, and housing," I said. "But with this much we could... Um, sorry. It's not my money or the city's."

"You got a good one," Warren replied. "Piper has been very charitable when commissioning deeply inappropriate art."

Piper tipped the chest's lid back on with a sly grin.

"Is it stolen?" That probably was not the thing I should have asked, because Piper instantly dropped his hand from mine.

"It's the fruits of my labor," Piper objected. "Spent way too much time on that ship, and there's not much to buy or give at sea."

"He helped guide the wind in the ship's sails," Warren explained. "Sometimes the threat of violence from pirates was used when anyone tried to shortchange him."

"Geez." I suddenly realized how close I was to pirates storming the city. "I got lucky, huh?"

"Oh no, not with this," Piper grinned. "That rat catcher reward was a deeply inflated wage."

"Then why did you demand... *You're a brat!*" I reached for him, and he skirted away, but it was useless since he never strayed far. I pinned an arm behind him so he'd stop moving, then looked at Warren. "Do you mind if I keep this pied piper?"

"All yours. We won't be back for a while," Warren said before his attention narrowed to his friend. "You happy here?"

It was a candid question, but Piper didn't seem surprised. Nor did he try to twist out of my hold. "Yes, thank you."

When I let go, they gave each other a quick hug before exchanging goodbyes. I expected that to be it, but then the other mage said the most curious thing. "If you come across the Wolf King, will you tell him I forgive him?"

Wait... Did they actually know the royals and the scale on which all their politics worked?

"I will," Piper said and waved Warren off. We silently watched as his friend rowed out, making a much quicker time of it without the heavy chest.

"You knew the Wolf King?" I finally asked.

"Not personally," Piper said casually. "I knew his predecessor through. Stars have no mercy on that soul."

Holy shit... how?

"Look at your face right now," Piper laughed.

"Are you fooling me?"

"No; your expression is hilarious."

"I meant—"

"I know what you meant," Piper interrupted. He wrapped his arms around me from behind and rested his head on my shoulder. "Doesn't matter what my story was; it matters what my story *is*. Here with you."

We went back to watching the coast and the ship on the horizon. Sails out, ready to catch the wind.

"Where does our adventure go next?" I asked.

"Home."

I snuggled under the sheets before opting to make the bed even cozier and pulled a blanket up from where it rested in a bundle near the bottom. Inadvertently, I had allowed the tiniest bit of the extra softness to cover Piper as he laid next to me.

"Stop giving me this," he objected and pushed the blanket back to my side. "I'm hot enough already."

"Yeah, you are," I said, and this time deliberately placed the blanket over his legs. "But what's mine is yours."

"Stop, it's not!" He laughed as he flung the blanket back to my side. "Behave, or I'm going to kick you out of bed."

"You can't kick a man out of his own bed." The fake horror in my tone didn't last as I directed Piper's mouth closer. "Please, I'll be good."

Our kiss was like lightning. A striking intensity that stole my breath as long as his mouth was cradled against mine.

"*Mmm*, when you kiss like that... I can't imagine you'd get kicked out of anyone's bed."

I smiled wordlessly as I righted the blanket, so it was smoothed out and *only* on my side.

"Hey..." There was a question in Piper's word. The actual definition was lost in the intent to have my focus. "You know I love you, right?"

His expression was hopeful, as if never wanting me to forget the truth under all of his goofing around.

"Yeah..." My heart seemed to skip a beat before pounding harder to catch up to the song that was falling for someone as wondrous as him. "I love you too."

"Forever, ever after?"

"And then some."

Discover Big Bad Magic In:

THE 8TH RANK

An enchanted wolf familiar. A noble thief. And a magic-fueled race to stop the murder of a queen.

Haunted by his missing memories, Mal wants answers. This Big Bad Wolf only knows he's been wrongfully made a villain. When a magic mirror shows Robin Hood is searching for him, Mal hopes this man might be his long-lost home.

Mal must stitch together the pieces of his reclaimed past to find out who Robin was to him. All signs point to Robin being his childhood friend, but Mal is interested in being more than just friends now. Thankfully, Mal's magical talents make him a valuable resource for any cause. And he's willing to dedicate himself to one man: Robin Hood.

Reunited in a hidden forest, Mal learns his desires to get closer aren't so unrequited after all. With the kingdom overrun with chaos, Mal and Robin's relationship is put to the test. Can they overcome the obstacles in their path to find their happily ever after?

Get ready for fairytales to collide **The 8th Rank** is the first in the spellbinding Big Bad Magic series. This fantasy novel features a cursed hero in search of redemption in a friends to lovers romance, ending with a happily ever after.

ABOUT THE AUTHOR

Rose Sinclair is the profane community leader who started with a blog in 2013. The biggest noise maker they spearheaded was a protest in 2015 that made GLADD step up for the wider LGBTQIA+ community, paving the way for future acceptance for people and on-screen TV representation. Before becoming a full-time writer, they popularized several terms, and set up a decentralized support system with a "Dear Abby" style approach. They are the author of HELLO WORLD, the BIG BAD MAGIC fantasy romance series, and plenty of other queer love stories.

Don't forget to drop your email at
RoseSinclair.com so you don't miss out on
any new releases and get exclusive free stories!